A Painful Dilemma

SCOTTISH WEREBEARS BOOK 5

LORELEI MOONE

Copyright © 2016 Lorelei Moone,
Cover art by germancreative
Published by eXplicitTales
All rights reserved.
ISBN: 9781913930202

CONTENTS

A Painful Dilemma   1

About the Author   96

PROLOGUE

Henry checked his watch and shook his head, even though there was nobody to see him do it. This was the last straw.

Here he was, on what looked to be a perfectly pleasant winter's day, spying on one of his own. And why? Because Adrian Blacke, self-appointed leader of the Alliance Council himself had ordered him to. *Just ensure our secrets are being kept,* Blacke had said. *He's never lived according to our customs, with our rules. There's no way of knowing if we can trust him.*

Nonsense.

Hadn't Matthew Argyle and the human woman, Leah Hudson, been through enough already?

After being abducted as a child and sent to live with strangers, finally, Matthew had found out the truth about himself. And clearly - if the activity going on inside was anything to go by - he'd found himself a mate as well. Good for him.

But if Blacke had his way, Henry would march in there and arrest both of them for violating the secrecy requirement all shifters are meant to live by. Fraternizing with humans was frowned upon in the best of circumstances, but recently Blacke had reached new heights of paranoia and decided to outlaw it completely.

What was the point of keeping their existence secret, if their main enemy, the Sons of Domnall knew all about them anyway? They were growing in numbers, organizing themselves, and turning more militant by the day. And by staying in the shadows, the shifters were playing right into their hands.

It was much easier to convince people to fear the unknown when nobody argued for the other side.

Henry had had these thoughts before, but the more he considered it, the more certain he'd become. Education was the way forward.

A far away rustle brought Henry back to reality. Was someone else watching?

He focused on pinpointing the noise, just across the other side of the backyard he'd been surveilling himself. This could not be a coincidence. Had Blacke sent out another Alliance agent?

Henry silently made his way around the boundary fence, while listening out for more sounds. No, the other spy was human. Bears would never be this obvious.

It didn't take him long to scale the fence, land on the other side and follow the retreating human female who had almost reached the back door of her house. Before she had the chance to see him, Henry grabbed the woman from behind and covered her mouth with his hand. She let out a muffled squeal and tried to struggle free, but it was no use.

"Make a move, and things will end badly for you," he whispered in her ear.

She soon stopped squirming.

"Okay, just don't hurt me," she said as Henry removed the hand from her mouth.

Henry kept her restrained with one arm, and with the other patted her down for weapons. She didn't carry any, but she did have a digital camera in her pocket, which Henry retrieved and switched on to inspect its contents.

So his instincts were right. He flipped through the pictures and found that they were shots of the exact scene he'd witnessed earlier, along with some very damning pictures of things that had happened before he'd even arrived at Leah Hudson's house.

This bumbling human, no doubt the collaborator one of the Sons of Domnall guys had referred to during his interrogation, had actually managed to get a picture of Matthew mid-shift. It was bad. If Blacke saw this, things would end badly for Matthew and his human mate.

Henry stuffed the camera into one of the pockets of his tactical vest and tied the woman's wrists up with one of the plastic restraints he always carried with him.

"Your mates ratted you out. You're coming with me now," Henry said.

The woman's eyes widened in shock, but she didn't say anything.

"What's your name?" he asked.

She remained silent.

"Very well, don't tell me."

Henry covered her mouth with a piece of duct tape and dragged her to the backdoor of the house she'd tried to enter earlier. He listened out for any activity but didn't hear any. The place was empty. On the way through the house, he picked up a few unopened envelopes from a sideboard. They were all addressed the same person: Caroline Pratt.

The few framed pictures on display showed the same woman, posing along with other people, some of which looked familiar to Henry. Sons of Domnall members already captured by the Alliance. That's all he needed to know.

Henry wasted no more time, just checked that the road was empty before getting her to the van and stuffing her in the back.

He might not have followed Blacke's orders exactly, but at least he had something to show for his little excursion to Gartcosh this afternoon. Just as well. He'd made up his mind earlier about what was the right way forward.

In time, if his plan worked out, perhaps this stupid war between the Sons and the shifters would pass, but for now, she was still the enemy. Henry wouldn't feel bad about locking her up at the base and later handing her over to Blacke and his men.

What he wouldn't do was hand over the pictures she'd taken earlier.

He was done spying on his own people, especially those who'd been through so much shit already, like Matthew Argyle. Henry had joined the Alliance because he wanted to make a difference; to make the world a safer place for shifters. Instead of simply following orders he didn't believe in anymore, he was going to start a movement of his own.

He locked the van and observed the outside of Leah Hudson's house for a moment. As much as he hated to interrupt the lovebirds, he couldn't leave without talking to at least Matthew first.

If Henry's new movement was to be a success, he needed to gather support. Who better to talk to than the man who inspired Henry's decision in the first place?

Henry picked the lock to the front door and waited inside the living room.

———— ♦ ————

It felt like hours before Henry noticed any sign of activity inside the human woman's house. He'd always been a patient man, so the wait didn't bother him as such. What bothered him was that he wasn't at all sure how to broach the subject he wanted to discuss.

And what if it wasn't Matthew Argyle who found him waiting in here, but the woman? He didn't want to panic anyone or create a scene. He just wanted to... What exactly *did* he want?

Henry wasn't sure, and time had run out to think about it any further, because a figure appeared in the doorway.

"Henry." Matt folded his arms.

"Matt. You know why they sent me here?" Henry asked.

"I can guess. And before you say anything else, no, you can't take her." Matt straightened himself further. He was on full alert, ready to defend his mate to the death if necessary.

Of course, Henry didn't make a move. That was not why he had come here.

"There's been a lot of enemy activity in the city, and everyone is on high alert," Henry tried to explain, but it didn't help get his point across.

"I don't care. I'm not going to let you take her."

Henry shook his head. It was only natural that Matt would be suspicious of his presence here. Even if he was planning to do nothing of the sort.

"Relax. I'm not going to take her." *Even if Blacke would have liked nothing better.* "The truth is, I'm not happy with the status-quo. What happened to you, here, it's not right. None of this is right."

This was not at all easy. Henry was used to being in control of himself and of any situation he got himself in. Years of Alliance experience had taught him to always prepare for whatever came next; to never follow impulse alone. Today marked a significant departure from said training.

"Okay... What are you trying to say exactly?" Matt still sounded suspicious - naturally. His body language was clear; as far as he knew, the threat was still very much present.

"I have a plan to make things right, but it's going to take time to set up."

"Shoot," Matt said.

Henry remembered his prisoner, out in the van. Perhaps if he started by explaining what had gone down earlier, he could win Matt's trust.

"Firstly, this is for you." Henry handed over the SD card he had taken from Caroline Pratt earlier.

It took a little explaining to get Matt to understand what had happened and how he'd got the SD card. Matt was obviously taken aback when he realized what Matt's prisoner had captured on camera. Luckily, the culprit was already under arrest so she wouldn't bother the two of them any longer.

Then it was time for Henry to bring up the one subject he had come here to discuss. His plans.

"I want to go public." Henry tried to gauge Matt's reaction. He looked surprised more than anything else.

"Think about it. None of this would have happened if people knew about our kind," Henry added.

Matt had a few more questions, which Henry tried to answer to the best of his ability. Yes, it went against the secrecy rules bears and other shifters had been following for centuries. Yes, the Alliance would oppose. But in the end, Henry believed it would be worth it.

"Okay, I'm in," Matt said after Henry had finished.

Finally, Henry could breathe a sigh of relief. His idea had legs, at least on the face of it.

Although he'd assured Matt that he wouldn't need anything other than his help when the time was right, there was no way of knowing how any of this would play out. Still, Henry's new movement had gained its first supporter.

CHAPTER ONE

Henry hadn't wanted a fight, but things had a way of escalating between him and Maggie.

"Why don't you trust me anymore?" Maggie folded her arms.

"Come on; it's not like that!" Henry argued, taking a step forward to rest his hand on Maggie's arm.

She pulled away just in time and shook her head. "Well, there's no other explanation. First, you go on the surveillance mission on your own, then you don't even involve me in the interrogation of that prisoner you took. Tell me, what am I supposed to think?"

Henry sighed. In a way, she was right. He *hadn't* wanted her to come along to Gartcosh to surveil Matt's house the other day. It's not that he didn't trust her, or didn't think she'd do a good job. Actually, he expected she'd do *too good* a job. She would have followed Blacke's orders to the letter, so they would have ended up with three prisoners, not just one. Caroline Pratt was a given, she was a Son's collaborator after all, but Maggie would have also rounded up Matt and Leah.

He and Maggie had been an item for years; Henry knew how she functioned.

As for the interrogation, he just couldn't risk Caroline cracking and mentioning the pictures she'd taken. Luckily, so far she seemed to hold up quite well and not said a word.

"Blacke gave me the order; it's only natural that I execute it," Henry excused his decision.

He had to come clean to her about what had happened, but with Maggie in the mood she was in right now, it wasn't the right time. She'd always been hot-blooded, and not particularly easy to reason with when she was ticked off.

"Did Blacke tell you not to take your partner along on the job?" Maggie demanded.

Henry remained quiet. Of course, he hadn't.

"I didn't think so."

She was hurt, obviously. And Henry couldn't blame her. But if there was one thing he had to give her credit for, she did take her work very seriously.

"Look, I didn't mean to step on your toes, but I can't have you questioning my operational decisions like this. When we're on the job, I'm in charge. That's just the way things are."

"Fine!" Maggie pressed her lips together. There was nothing agreeable about her body language.

"Now, shall we have breakfast? Wouldn't want to be late for work."

Maggie shrugged and marched out of their bedroom. Although he'd pulled the seniority card on her, this argument was far from over.

Today was going to be a long day.

———— ◆ ————

For much of the day, Maggie made it a point to steer clear of Henry, which was just as well. They weren't hiding their relationship as such, but they made it a point to always stay professional at work.

Henry liked to think of himself as a fair and capable leader. His agents trusted him - most of the time, in the case of Maggie - and he ensured not to give preferential treatment to his mate. Plus, bears weren't the sharing sort. They didn't wear their hearts on their sleeve like wolves seemed to do. In his unit, one's private life was just that: private.

Before lunch, Henry interrogated his latest prisoner - Caroline Pratt - some more. Nothing came out of it, just as he had come to expect from most of the Sons of Domnall members. Especially those that seemed to be authority figures of some sort were especially tight-lipped. Caroline's demeanor, as well as her role in the attempted second kidnapping of Matthew Argyle, made Henry suspect she wasn't just an informant, but perhaps a faction leader.

Then again, she wasn't in the loop on a great many Sons activities at all, or she might have already known who or what Matt was.

Either way, it was time to close the file on her and send her and the other prisoners across to Stirling, where the Alliance Headquarters were located. Henry wrote up a sanitized version of the events leading up to Caroline's capture, whatever little details he gathered during the interrogation, and that was that. Case closed. He'd inform Blacke's people shortly.

Once that was done, he grabbed a fresh sheet of paper and started to brainstorm about something else entirely. He'd had an epiphany outside Matt's house that day, but he hadn't taken the time to really think about it in depth. If he was going to set up a movement to counter Blacke's Alliance, he couldn't just wing it.

Who would be onboard with his idea? Anyone who - like Matt - had paired up with another species, obviously.

How would he find these people and convince them, though? Considering how notoriously secretive bears were about their personal lives, identifying potential recruits would be very difficult indeed. Henry didn't even know enough about his own team's relationships to be able to make an educated guess about whom to approach with his idea.

There had to be two recruitment phases: a slow start, relying on word of mouth, followed by a public call for support once they were ready to reveal themselves. Once his new movement was ready to go public, they might just attract complete strangers who agreed with Henry's ideology.

Henry sat back and looked at the sheet in front of him. Other than Matt, he hadn't been able to add a single name to his list of potential supporters. He crushed the paper into a ball and threw it in the trash.

What he was planning was big, too big for one person to orchestrate. He didn't just need supporters; he needed a partner to help him organize everything.

Henry looked up and saw her walk in. Maggie. Was she still angry at him? If he brought it up, would she be his partner in this new venture as well? There was only one way to find out.

"You ready?" she asked.

Henry glanced at his watch; five-thirty.

"Yeah, why not." He pushed the Caroline Pratt's dossier aside and got up. "Hey, how about we go out tonight? Somewhere nice."

Maggie cocked her head to the side. She pursed her lips like she often did when she was mulling something over.

Definitely still annoyed about this morning Henry thought.

"We'll go anywhere you like," he added.

Maggie smiled, and Henry knew he'd won at least the first battle of the evening.

———◆———

Henry waited until the waiter left before broaching the subject that had been on his mind most of the day.

"The work we do..." he started, then looked up to find Maggie already staring at him intently. "Do you ever wonder if we're doing all we can?"

"We're making a difference, aren't we? Only a few years ago, we had no idea about the threat against us posed by the Sons of Domnall. Now we're hot on their trail and arresting new people all the time."

"True, we're making progress. I do wonder sometimes if we're doing the right thing."

Maggie's eyes narrowed. "What are you trying to say?"

"The other day, the surveillance order on Matt Argyle," Henry said, hoping against hope that she wouldn't see this as an invitation to start this morning's argument all over again.

She paused for a moment.

"What about it?"

"It just didn't feel right. He's one of us, not the enemy." Henry ran his hand through his hair.

"God, is that why you didn't want me to go? Because you weren't sure it was the right call?" Maggie sat back and observed him for a moment. "You got an order; you followed it. I honestly don't see the problem. And if he isn't following the rules, he might as well be the enemy."

"You really think that?" Henry asked. This conversation wasn't going as he had hoped.

"I can't believe you're even asking me this. We signed up for this thing for the same reason: to keep our people safe. Things are getting worse. Disappearances, even murders. As many Sons members as we've caught, we have no way of knowing how many more are out there."

"True."

"It's not rocket science. Keep our true nature a secret from humanity. What's so hard in that?"

Henry sighed. Maggie was a strong woman. That was one of her qualities which he'd always admired. The downside was that she could be incredibly stubborn. There was no convincing her of something she didn't already believe in. There was little point in discussing this matter any further.

"You're right. It's quite simple," he said. "Oh, the food is here."

Henry smiled at the waiter as he brought out their plates. Steak, medium-rare. Just what he needed.

He glanced over at Maggie again, who looked equally pleased to see the food.

For the rest of the meal, Henry didn't bring up his doubts about Blacke's policies anymore. It seemed Maggie was equally content to leave the topic behind as Henry was. Perhaps it had been the wrong time to discuss it, but at the very least she wasn't angry anymore about being excluded from the surveillance job.

As pleasant as the meal had been, the evening left Henry with a bitter taste in his mouth. By the time they'd gone to bed, doubts had started to overwhelm him. He turned to look at Maggie beside him, her eyes closed and features completely relaxed. How different she looked when she was asleep.

She wasn't onboard with his idea. This was a major setback, and unlike how Henry had hoped for things to turn out. But it was normal for couples to disagree on things. They had to get past it.

Somehow, Henry had to figure out a way to start the new movement himself, without her help. Blacke needed to be stopped somehow before he went too far, no matter what Maggie believed. They were a team in the office, a team at home, most of the time. But this was something he had to do for his own satisfaction and beliefs.

He needed to come up with a solid plan and gather support beyond Matt all on his own. Hopefully, then Maggie would see that Henry was right and join him after all.

CHAPTER TWO

This was not what Gail imagined her new job would be like. Not at all.

She held on tighter to the pile of document folders as she tried to keep pace with her new boss, Adrian Blacke, on the way to the holding cells located in the basement of the Alliance headquarters in Stirling, Scotland.

It was like a typical scene from a coming of age chick flick, only she refused to play the part of the clumsy heroine who would drop all her papers as her boss lost patience with her. That's not who she wanted to be.

Who *did* she want to be? Gail wasn't sure.

She followed Blacke through the heavy, reinforced doors, through the long corridor, stealing glances through the narrow windows in the cell doors. Inside each of them sat someone who had been deemed a danger to the shifter world, whether through threatening or violent behavior or by simply breaking one or more Alliance rules. It seemed like the latter group made up most of the prisoners here.

Their footsteps echoed against the concrete of the hallway as they made their way further into the belly of what her colleagues referred to as 'the dungeon'; a fitting name indeed for a place as unpleasant as this.

"Let's see what old man Campbell has to say for himself today," Blacke muttered.

After just over a week on the job, Gail knew better than to respond. Blacke had a habit of talking to himself when it was just the two of them. As if she wasn't even present.

They approached the cell where Lee Campbell was being kept - just across from his son Gareth who had been captured at the same time apparently. His cell was one of the few with a dedicated guard; he was one of the most valuable prisoners here.

Most of the Sons of Domnall members they had captured were just small-time soldiers, but Lee Campbell was something else entirely. He was a leader of some sort, though his exact rank wasn't yet known.

Blacke nodded at the guard, who unlocked the heavy door and stepped aside. Gail followed her boss inside the cell, though it made her skin crawl to be here. This, coming down here, was one of the more unpleasant parts of her job.

She couldn't be sure what Blacke was planning for today, but his personal interrogations of Campbell had turned nastier and nastier over time. The more Campbell kept quiet, the more determined Blacke had become to make him talk.

"Morning," Adrian Blacke said, his voice low and sinister.

Campbell, who was merely sitting on the basic cot in the corner of his otherwise sparse cell, looked up. His eyes were blank like he wasn't actually present. His face was an unhealthy shade of grey, and the bags under his eyes seemed to darken with every passing day.

His deterioration wasn't all that surprising, considering they had kept him locked up in this windowless basement for weeks now. In an attempt to break his resolve, Blacke had instructed the guards to wake Campbell every two hours throughout the night and put him on a severely restricted diet.

Gail shuddered at the sight of Blacke, who continued to glare at the miserable looking man. Some days, the prisoners seemed more approachable and sympathetic than her boss did.

Blacke snapped his fingers, jerking Gail into action.

"Yes, sir?" she asked.

"A chair. Get me a chair."

Gail turned on her heel, eager to get out of the dingy cell, but her relief was cut short by the guard outside who had already arranged for a chair. Damn.

She dragged it inside with one hand, the steel feet making an awful kind of noise scraping over the bare concrete of the floor.

Blacke sat down without acknowledging her.

"Let's try something new today, shall we?" Blacke said. "We'll step things up, as they say."

Gail's insides twisted painfully. She really wasn't keen to find out what Blacke had in mind.

"Get me Agent Dumbarton," Blacke spoke in a low growl.

Gail nodded and finally made her escape from the cell. This was bad, very bad. Dumbarton was mean. One of those guys who didn't think twice before getting physical. Calling him into an interrogation could only mean one thing: Blacke planned to make good on his threats; he was finally going to have the prisoner tortured.

With every passing step, back past all those cells, through the doors and up the stairs, Gail couldn't shake the feeling of dread that her realization had inspired. She didn't want to be here.

That man, Campbell no doubt was the enemy, as were the rest of the Sons of Domnall. He'd kill her and everyone in this building if he had the chance. But this went too far. If they did this, they'd sink to his level and justify his beliefs that shifters were dangerous and needed to be rooted out.

Her hands trembled as she opened the door leading to the main floor where all the agents had their desks. It didn't take her long to spy Dumbarton in a crowd hanging around the coffeemaker. He was the loudest of the lot.

"Agent Dumbarton," Gail addressed him, attempting to sound a lot more confident than she felt. "Mr. Blacke needs you in the dungeon. Cell 27."

Dumbarton gave her one of those looks. The ones that make you feel dirty and violated. "Sure thing, darling. Anything for you."

Some of the other agents chuckled. Pigs, the lot of them.

She didn't want to wait for what else he would say, instead made a run for the exit. Whether Blacke wanted her back down there or not, she didn't care. She wasn't willing to watch what was going to happen next.

Outside, the grey skies perfectly matched her mood. The only noise around was the groundskeeper who operated a leaf blower to clear away the last fallen leaves of autumn.

The Alliance headquarters was situated in a strange looking mansion built in the 1920s by Blacke's grandfather. Ever since he'd taken over control of the Alliance Council, this place - which thanks to its concrete and steel exterior looked more like a bunker or a prison than a luxury country retreat - had been used to hold council meetings and store prisoners taken by the various Alliance branch offices.

It was ugly, as were most of the people inside.

Gail took a deep breath, but it didn't help calm her nerves. The hum of the leaf blower stopped, as Gerry, the caretaker retrieved a pack of cigarettes from his pocket and lit one. Perhaps that would help.

"Gerry, excuse me," Gail called out to him.

He looked up, as though surprised that anyone was talking to him at all.

She approached him, her knees weak as she did so. "May I have one?"

"Sure." He retrieved the crumpled packet and held it up for her.

"Thank you," she said.

He offered her a light and continued his work straightaway. Like most bears, Gerry was a man of few words.

Gail walked back towards the building, hoping that standing closer to its walls would offer some shelter against the sharp wintery breeze. She inhaled deeply, waiting for the smoke to relax her. It did nothing of the sort.

All it did was made her cough and feel nauseous. What a ridiculous idea. Why would a cigarette help her when she didn't even smoke? She put it out against the bottom of her shoe and leaned back against the cold concrete with her head down and eyes shut.

Gail wasn't sure how long she remained like that for, only that the sound of an approaching vehicle made her look up again. Black, windowless, Ford Transit. All of the HQ agents were on site, so this could only mean one thing: a transport bringing with it more unfortunate souls to be forgotten in the dungeon.

She didn't want to see who was being held in the back. She didn't want to think about what would happen to them, but rather than run inside, something made her stick around and watch.

The driver's side door opened, and her heart all but stopped.

Gail had never seen the man before during her time here. His broad shoulders looked like they could carry the world on them. He was most definitely a brown bear, bigger and stronger than her own subspecies. Although she knew nothing about him, when he turned around she could see in his eyes that he was different from all the guys working inside. He was meant to be hers. She could feel it.

Gail tried to swallow the last remnants of that horrible cigarette and dusted herself off.

"Hey," she said, but it came out all hoarse at first. "Hey!"

The man, who had already walked around to the back of his van, looked up.

"Can I help you?" Gail asked.

"Prisoner transport." The man barely acknowledged her presence beyond that, instead unlocking the backdoor of his vehicle.

Gail nodded. She did vaguely remember Blacke

discussing an upcoming transport with other people in the office. Still, it was infuriating that he wasn't paying any attention to her at all. He was her mate; she just *knew* it. However, he seemed to be completely oblivious.

"Name? I'm Gail McPherson, by the way. Mr. Blacke's assistant."

That last bit of information seemed to sink in, because the man stopped what he was doing again and turned to face her.

"Agent Weston. Your boss is expecting me."

"I see..." Gail frowned. Why couldn't things just be simple? Not only was she stuck doing a job that wasn't at all how she thought it was going to be, here was a guy who didn't behave in the least how he was meant to. She'd heard about the instant attraction bears experience when they are confronted with their true mate. It was always mutual. Why wasn't it mutual now?

"I will let him know you're here," Gail said.

She paused for another moment, only to find that so-called Agent Weston was intent on ignoring her presence. *Fine!* Off she went to notify her boss of the arrival of Weston and his transport.

Perhaps once he was done doing the job he had come here for he would be more open to converse with her.

CHAPTER THREE

Henry was still in shock when he led Caroline Pratt into the Alliance Headquarters. That woman, Gail McPherson, who had introduced herself as Adrian Blacke's assistant, had awoken things in him he hadn't felt before. A connection. A certainty that he was meant to be with her.

But that couldn't be. He had chosen Maggie as his mate already, someone he'd known and worked with for years.

This is just a silly infatuation, he told himself. *There's no way this is real.*

Perhaps it was due to the recent disagreements between Maggie and him, most notably their differing views on their work. That had to be it.

Every relationship took work and dedication. Everyone had doubts sometimes. He just had to make sure not to give in to them.

"Prisoner transfer from Glasgow," Henry told the man manning the front desk. "Mr. Blacke is expecting me."

"Hold on, let me check." The man picked up the phone on the table in front of him and dialed a few numbers. "All right, you can go straight down. Is it just the one prisoner?"

Henry shook his head. There were more in the van. "Two more."

"Very well. Bill, give us a hand here, will ya?" The agent called out to one of his colleagues who had just passed through the double doors at the other end of the entrance hall.

The other guy, Bill, nodded and approached Henry.

"This one and two more prisoners as requested by Mr. Blacke," the man behind the desk clarified.

"Understood. Follow me."

Bill led Henry along with his prisoner to another, less

impressive door in the corner. Behind it was the staircase leading into the basement. They walked in silence, almost all the way to the end of the long corridor, cells on either side. One of the doors opened, and that same woman from before, Gail, almost ran into Henry.

"Careful, there," he mumbled, as he reached out to steady her by her arm.

Their eyes met, and he felt it again. The pull, the strange attraction he'd never felt before. *You're mine.* He immediately pulled his hand back again. How awkward. Had she noticed him stare?

"Excuse me," she whispered. She shot a cold stare at Henry's companion and marched off back in the direction of the staircase. Like she couldn't wait to get out of here. Obviously, he'd made her uncomfortable with his weird behavior.

"Nice one, aye. I wouldn't mind bumping into that myself," Bill remarked and stopped for a moment, looking back at Gail as she walked away.

It was distasteful. Henry balled his fists and took a deep breath. There was no point getting into a confrontation with this guy. And over what? Some misplaced feeling of protectiveness towards a woman who wasn't even his to protect. What a mess.

"Let's do this," Henry grumbled under his breath while prodding Caroline in the back to make her walk faster.

"What?" Bill asked, then shrugged when Henry didn't reply. "Here we are. You can leave the prisoner in here. I'll open up a couple more cells for the others."

"Great. I'll be right back." Henry left Caroline behind and turned back immediately. His feet seemed to carry him in a hurry back to the door at the end of the hall, up the stairs, and through the entrance hall back outside. As though he was stuck in a trance.

The fresh air helped clear his head. He was just going to do what he had come here for and stop obsessing about that woman.

With everything that was already on his mind, this was the last thing he needed.

Luckily, it seemed she had read his mind, because he didn't run into her again.

Within little under an hour, he had delivered the remaining prisoners and handed over their paperwork as well. He'd also been taken in to see Mr. Blacke himself, who questioned him on his findings regarding Matt Argyle's conduct. All in order, Henry had said.

That's as much as he was willing to divulge, and luckily, Blacke hadn't pushed him further.

If only Blacke knew what Henry was planning... For now, though, Henry's senior position in the Glasgow office afforded him a certain amount of trust from the normally quite suspicious Alliance Council leader.

Henry made a quick exit as soon as everything was settled. No matter how hard he tried throughout the lonely drive back, he couldn't get Gail out of his mind. Raven black hair, dark brown, nearly black eyes, and flawless olive skin. She was something else. When he closed his eyes, it was as though he could catch her scent again.

How was he meant to resist such temptation? When every cell in his body seemed to ache for her. He wasn't a womanizer. He couldn't betray Maggie.

Finally, about halfway through the drive, he couldn't take it anymore. Rather than continue straight to Glasgow, he took the next exit and just kept on driving. Through fields and small towns and villages, until he found himself at the shores of a lake. That's where he pulled over and got out.

It was getting late, the sun was setting, and a frosty wind battered the landscape.

He closed his eyes and inhaled deeply. The cold air stung against his nostrils and helped him gain clarity. His bear wasn't happy, and there was only one way to appease him right now.

About three hundred feet from where he'd parked the

car were some pine woods. They'd provide shelter for what he had to do next.

As soon as Henry reached the first trees, he started to unzip his jacket. The rest of his clothes followed soon after.

It was freezing, but if he was going to make it back home after this without exposing himself, getting undressed first was as necessary as it was uncomfortable. He folded everything into a neat little bundle and left it underneath some fallen needles and branches.

Then he let the animal side take over. As soon as his fur had grown, he felt better. Now he was protected against the elements and ready to wander through the pine forest. He had a lot to think about.

What was it about that woman that the thought of her wouldn't leave him alone?

And was there any hope for his plans to tell the world about shifters? If Blacke got wind of what he was up to, he'd have him locked away and the key thrown away.

How would he get the support he'd need to execute his plans?

Even in bear form, glimpses of Gail kept popping into his mind. Why? Why couldn't he focus properly?

He wasn't sure how long he'd been running for, but in the distance, a familiar sight showed up, barely visible through the fog that had set in.

The large sprawling farm he'd grown up on. Home.

Why had he come here? He wasn't sure. But now that he was here, he might as well pop in.

There was a familiar scent in the air; his mom's famous pot roast. Was she expecting someone? It seemed like an odd meal to cook just for oneself.

Ever since his dad's passing, she'd lived alone on this large property. Henry wasn't sure how she managed everything, but every offer he'd made for her to move in with him and Maggie had fallen on deaf ears.

"Son," it was unmistakably her, who called out to him

from the front door. "I've been expecting you." She stepped ahead into the light flooding the porch. Every time he saw her, her hair seemed to grow more white, her skin more fragile.

Henry hesitated. How was that possible? He hadn't even known himself that he would end up here.

"Mom. Thanks, but I won't stay long. Maggie will be wondering where I am."

"You didn't bring her along?" His mom reached out for him, and he leaned down, allowing her to pat the thick fur on his back.

Henry shook his head. "Just me."

"Very well. Why don't you freshen up? Dinner's almost ready."

Henry nodded and walked in through the spacious entrance, up the broad stairs leading to his old bedroom. Inside, he found a pair of jeans and a chunky hand knitted pullover already laid out for him. With a sigh, he let go of his bear and morphed back into his human self.

A heavy feeling overwhelmed him immediately. What was it? Sadness? Guilt?

The wooden steps creaked underneath his bare feet as he made his way down.

When he entered the kitchen, his mom was already waiting, roasting tray in hand.

"I hope you're hungry." She smiled at him. "Son. What's troubling you? You don't look yourself today."

"How did you know I was coming?" Henry wondered aloud.

"I had a feeling... ever since I woke up this morning to milk the cows. I suppose a mother just knows."

That didn't make much sense to Henry, but he didn't want to question it anymore.

He followed her into the dining room and sat down at the large rectangular table. This place had always seemed disproportionate, too spacious for a couple and their only son. Now it was even odder, with his dad gone.

She started carving the meat and served him first, then herself.

"Eat. You look like you need it."

Henry nodded. He must have run quite a distance to get here. He wasn't even sure where he'd parked the car exactly. He'd have to find his way back by scent.

His mom observed him as he ate, taking only a couple of bites of the food herself. After a while, he couldn't stand being watched so closely anymore and put his knife and fork down.

"Something's on your mind," she said before Henry had the chance to say something himself.

He sat back and sighed. A lot of things were on his mind; she was right about that.

"You know, the work I do..." he started.

His mom pushed her plate away and folded her hands, resting them on the rough wood.

"To help our kind. With the Alliance," she responded.

"Right. Well lately, I wonder if it's really helping."

"I see. Do you want to quit; is that it?"

Henry shook his head. "No, I just want to make a difference, like I had hoped to."

"And you think the Alliance isn't succeeding at that?"

"I wonder if they're going down a wrong path. Something that'll do us more harm than our enemies are already doing."

"How so?"

"Did you know we're arresting our own kind now?" Henry also pushed his plate away. Talking about all this had ruined his appetite.

"For what?"

"For what... For taking a mate of a different species, that's the latest one. Did you know they're proposing to implant all newborn cubs with trackers now also? We haven't received the orders yet, but they're coming. They say it's for our safety, in case one of them gets taken, but who is to say it's not to keep tabs on them as well?"

His mom frowned. "Things have really changed, haven't they?" She shook her head.

"They have," Henry agreed. "I'm not sure I want any more part of it."

"Son. Only you can decide what to do. You must follow your instincts."

"Lately, I've been wondering if perhaps a lot of our problems wouldn't be solved if we started living out in the open."

His mom was silent for a moment. "Humans are afraid of what they don't understand."

"Exactly. If we can make them understand, through education, and dialogue, they'd have nothing to be afraid of anymore."

She shook her head again. "I don't know."

"We're not living in the Middle Ages anymore. Human society is more tolerant now than it has ever been."

"You know better. It's hard to know what things are like outside these walls."

"I just don't know where to begin yet to make this happen."

She looked up and smiled at him. "You'll think of something. You always do."

Henry smiled back at her. It was good, being able to talk openly of all he'd been thinking about. He had hoped to have this conversation with Maggie, but obviously, that wasn't an option just yet; not until he had a solid plan in place.

CHAPTER FOUR

Ever since Blacke had mentioned the upcoming surprise visit to the Glasgow Alliance office, Gail had been struggling to keep her excitement under control. That's where the guy, Agent Weston, was based. The prospect of seeing him again made her giddy like a schoolgirl.

And perhaps, this time, he'd be on the same page and feel their connection as well.

She tried her best to keep her expectations in check, but it was no use.

Throughout the drive, she found it increasingly difficult to concentrate on the actual task at hand; organizing the documentation Blacke wanted to distribute regarding his latest pet project; a nationwide tracking program for young shifters. Project Safeguard, as he called it.

She had personally sent out memos to all the Alliance branches in the country a week ago. But that wasn't enough for Black, who insisted they must visit at least the nearest Alliance offices in person to ensure everyone's full participation.

Gail hadn't been keen for this new program to be rolled out. As much as Blacke insisted that his intentions were to track youngsters only in case they were reported missing by their parents, Gail couldn't shake the feeling that Project Safeguard could easily be misused as well.

She simply didn't trust Blacke. Gail glanced over at him sitting in the backseat of the spacious sedan beside her. He was furiously scribbling down notes of some sort. Preparing a speech, probably.

No matter what she thought about the tracker project, he was going ahead with it, and she had no say in the matter. At least, it meant she had an excuse to see that guy again.

It had only been a few days since they'd first run into each other at HQ, but she'd had a hard time thinking about anything else but that first meeting. Agent Weston had infiltrated her every waking moment and some non-waking ones as well.

By the time the car turned off the motorway and entered the city, her heart was racing so much, it made her feel light-headed. She looked out the window, but couldn't properly focus on the buildings and streets they passed by. It all merged into a blur.

Fifteen minutes later, they stopped in front of an empty-looking, dilapidated building. Once you'd seen one Alliance branch office, you'd seen them all; that's what the agents at HQ had said. It was located in an old warehouse in what looked to be an old industrial estate. It had been populated during a time when the Alliance favored discretion over anything else, and completely unlike the HQ which looked a lot more intimidating.

The driver opened the door for Blacke, leaving Gail to get out from her side on her own. She quickly gathered all the paperwork off the seat and rushed to get to the front door and pressed the buzzer.

"Identify yourself, and state your purpose," a crackly female voice answered.

"Mr. Blacke, official Council business," Gail responded.

The door opened with a loud click, and she entered to hold it open for her boss, who was right behind her by now.

In front of them, a woman in full combat gear appeared. "Welcome, Sir," she said. "Shall I assemble everyone inside?"

Blacke nodded, barely slowing down on his way inside. The woman vanished as quickly as she had appeared, meanwhile Gail just tried to keep up with her boss, who clearly knew exactly where he was headed even if she didn't.

They soon entered an office space that looked quite

similar to the one at HQ, though obviously not as grand and well-equipped. Half a dozen men and two women gathered around Blacke and Gail in a semi-circle.

"Welcome, Mr. Blacke, Sir," a familiar voice spoke behind them.

Gail could hardly contain her excitement. Agent Weston.

He nodded at her boss but didn't acknowledge her at all. Damn. So she was still the only one who could feel the attraction.

"Weston. Good, you're here. I have important matters to discuss. The files," Blacke turned to Gail, both his eyebrows raised expectantly.

Shit, the papers she'd been organizing. Gail shuffled through the things she'd carried inside and located the neat packets she'd prepared in the car. She handed them out to everyone in the room, finishing with Agent Weston. He still barely looked at her.

What the hell?

As soon as everyone had the documentation for Project Safeguard in front of them, Blacke started talking. He started off with the threat the Sons posed, about disappearances, and all that stuff Gail had heard so many times before. She retreated to a quiet corner and ignored Blacke's speech.

To keep from obsessing about Agent Weston too much, she started to read the top sheet of the papers she was still carrying. It was the handwritten notes Blacke had made in the car.

Phase 1: Project Safeguard encourages families to volunteer for trackers (Blood & DNA testing as part of qualification process).

Phase 2: Document families in detail, sending in teams as necessary to investigate their background and family tree.

Phase 3: Classify everyone according to new points system (still to be devised, but non-participation in Phase 1 should count as a red flag), grading the purity of their bloodline. Refer to DNA tests carried out in Phase 1.
Phase 4: Searchable database.
Phase 5: Compulsory trackers for high-risk families.
Phase 6: Activate audio transmission.

Underneath it was an incomplete flowchart with notes scribbled in the side, presumably behaviors Blacke didn't approve of, which he intended to record as part of the grading system.

Gail couldn't believe what she was reading. What he was proposing today was just the start of a much bigger, much more nefarious operation. Blacke was planning to divide up the shifter population, singling out families whose lineage he considered impure. To what end?

Didn't their kind have enough to worry about already, considering they were being hunted to death by the Sons of Domnall?

It was then that a single word in Blacke's speech caught Gail's attention. *Purity.*

She listened up just in time to hear him instruct the agents to start rounding up mixed couples in their jurisdiction.

"We've let these high risk behaviors slide for too long. But the shifter world is in crisis, ladies and gentlemen! We cannot afford to be so lax anymore."

Gail observed the crowd. Some, like the woman who had received them earlier, were nodding in agreement, while some others just seemed to be less convinced.

This isn't right. This just isn't right, Gail thought.

She felt a stare bore into her from across the room. Agent Weston. This was the first time she'd made proper eye-contact with the man. He was infuriatingly, distractingly handsome. Despite her concerns about Blacke's plans, she couldn't help but feel just a little bit excited to finally have Weston's full attention.

No, it's not right, a voice seemed to say in her head.

I can hear you, Gail thought.

Yes.

Someone has to do something about this. Stop him before he goes too far. Gail formulated the thought before even considering if she could trust him. Of course, she could, he was her mate after all. The feeling had to be mutual too; that's why he was in her head.

Mated couples could hear each other's thoughts; that's what all the stories said. Such is the connection when you find the one fate has picked out for you. Not that Gail personally knew a couple who could communicate telepathically, but that didn't make the stories any less true.

We have to do something. Agent Weston turned around to face the female agent who had greeted them before.

Before Gail could communicate anything else, she felt that their connection was broken. An immense sense of loss overwhelmed her, like a part of herself had gone missing. *What the hell had just happened?*

"Keep up the good work!" Blacke nodded at the crowd and turned around to join Gail.

"If we hurry, we can make it to Edinburgh and back before nightfall," Blacke muttered.

Shit, she couldn't leave just yet, could she? This thing with Agent Weston was still unresolved. How could she go without talking to him properly? When would she see him again?

Gail turned to find him looking at her again, and immediately she felt more reassured.

Go. I'll be in touch.

She nodded subtly, hopefully subtly enough that nobody else could see.

There was no choice but to do what she was told right

now. She didn't want to attract her boss's suspicion.

Before she had the chance to say or do anything else, Blacke had ushered her out of the room, down the hall and out of the building.

"We'll need another five information packs for Edinburgh," he said while getting into the back seat of the waiting car.

"Yes, sir."

The driver got in as well, and they pulled away swiftly, back-tracking their way through the same streets as before until they reached the motorway.

It had been a long day. The visit to Edinburgh was short, and the reaction of the agents there largely the same as in Glasgow. Some seemed convinced, others, not so much. Yet nobody argued or protested.

While she tried to stay alert, to assess which of the agents seemed to take issue with Blacke's proposals, but all the while her mind was a couple of hundred miles away. Weston. She didn't even know his first name yet, and at the same time, the connection they'd felt had been undeniable this time.

Once they got back to the Alliance Headquarters, it was pitch dark outside. Blacke was unstoppable, though. Now that he had taken the first step and announced his plans to the two nearest offices, he wasn't ready to slow down.

"We fly out to London in the morning; book us some tickets," he ordered.

Gail's heart sank. London? She couldn't leave now, not when Weston was about to make contact with her. She paused for a moment. There was no other choice; she couldn't go.

"Umm, Sir?"

"What is it?" He frowned impatiently. Blacke wasn't used to having someone question him.

"I was wondering if I might stay behind. My father hasn't been doing well, and I'd hate to have something happen to him while I'm away." Gail felt bad having to use her dad as an excuse to get out of a work trip, but it had been the only excuse she could think of.

Blacke sighed. "Family is important. Very well. I'll have Agent Finch accompany me to London." Despite the words of understanding, he sounded displeased. Had her reason for staying back been any less important, she might have backed down immediately.

Gail smiled. "Thank you, Sir. I'll book your tickets immediately."

"Just don't let this become too regular. I need someone I can depend on. Occasional travel is part of the job, understood?"

"Understood, sir."

Gail breathed a sigh of relief as she returned to her desk to make the necessary travel arrangements. She could only hope that while Blacke was away, Weston would make good on his promise to get in touch.

Whatever plans he had to *do something* about Blacke's new project were only part of the reason of course. Really, Gail was just desperate to see Agent Weston again. Perhaps if they found themselves alone...

CHAPTER FIVE

Henry couldn't believe what had happened.

Just like that, during Blacke's short announcement, everything had changed. The Alliance Council leader had lost his mind; that much was clear. But at the same time, his words had presented Henry with a huge opportunity.

The tracker project was on. Although Henry had no intention of actually implanting young shifters with GPS transmitters as instructed, he was going to make sure to publicize the project as much as possible. He would talk to every shifter family he could get in contact with, in the hopes that most of them would be as suspicious as he had been when he first heard about it.

At the same time, the second announcement that it was now open season on mixed couples had even more potential. It had been only a few days since he had realized mixed couples were the ones who had most to gain if he started a counter-movement to Blacke's Alliance. He just didn't know how to get in touch with them.

If the Alliance started investigating people's private lives to the extent that Blacke intended, he would come across plenty of potential recruits for his new movement.

This wasn't without risk, though. He would have to figure out a way that he could identify these potential targets, and then keep them safe without Blacke or anyone else finding out what he was up to.

And then there was the other thing. The voice in his head. The connection he'd made with Gail. Completely by chance, he'd potentially found the partner he'd yearned for.

Of course, he still had to talk to her about everything, but he was certain she'd join him. He'd felt her disgust, her outrage, as if it were his own.

Their relationship would be completely professional, of

course. He'd have to find a way to keep his straying mind under control around her. Perhaps that would get easier in time. But he did need the help, and who better to have on his side than an insider in Blacke's own office?

It was perfect.

For the rest of the day, Henry was in a better mood than he'd been for weeks. He whistled to himself while planning to promote Project Safeguard, even writing up a flyer he wanted to get printed and distributed among the local shifter population.

On the surface, Blacke would be pleased with his efforts. Henry intended to be his star agent going forward. A true believer in his crazy ideas. The Glasgow office would lead the way and become an example throughout the Alliance.

When the time would come to reveal his new movement, Henry's betrayal would sting even deeper. How he looked forward to that.

"You're awfully cheerful today," Maggie remarked.

How long had she been standing next to him?

Henry shrugged. "Just getting on with work. Hey, could you get someone to run over to the printers and get these leaflets made up?" He handed her the sample he'd printed out himself.

Maggie paused. "Okay..."

"Oh, and tomorrow I was thinking of taking some time out to visit the farm to check up on mom," Henry added.

"You think that's wise? With everything we've got going on?" Maggie questioned him.

His good mood soured almost immediately. Why did she have to do this?

"You don't have to come. I only have one mother, though, don't I?" It wasn't fair for him to be too annoyed since his visit to his mom was mostly a ruse, but what if it hadn't been? What if he'd planned to go there purely out of concern for her?

Henry took a deep breath and bit his tongue. This

wasn't the time to argue.

"Fine." Maggie shrugged and held up the print-out Henry had just given her. "I'll get this done then."

Henry nodded and focused once more on the paperwork ahead of him, even if his mind was struggling to get back on task.

The following morning, Henry didn't bother coming into the office. After saying his goodbyes to Maggie at home, he made the drive up north straight away, heading for Stirling. Throughout the night, he'd been mulling over various ideas for getting Gail out of the office without raising suspicion in her colleagues, especially Blacke.

In the end, he'd decided to try the least invasive option first. Considering she was Blacke's assistant, chances were she'd answer his phone calls for him. If Blacke actually did answer, he'd report on progress with Project Safeguard instead.

As soon as he had the front gate of the large compound the Alliance Headquarters were situated in within his sights, he pulled over onto the soft verge. Henry took out his phone and dialed the number.

"Hello?" A male voice answered. The guy who manned the front desk, probably.

"Agent Weston for Mr. Blacke."

Just like that, the man had put through Henry's call. Once again, there were certain advantages to his position within the Alliance.

"Mr. Blacke's office," a female voice said after only two rings.

It was her. It had to be.

"Weston here."

"Oh!" Was that surprise in her voice? Shock? He *had* told her he'd be in touch.

"Can I speak freely?"

"Uh, okay..."

"Is there some way you can get out of the office to talk?" Henry asked.

"I..." Gail cleared her throat, then continued in a much firmer tone, as though someone had just walked in on her. "I'm afraid Mr. Blacke is not available this week. Perhaps there's something I can help you with in the meantime?"

"How about you take an early lunch? Go for a refreshing walk through the grounds. I'll find you."

"No problem. I'll wait for your call." With that, she hung up.

They were on.

Although the road Henry's car was parked on was quiet, almost abandoned, he couldn't risk leaving his car here. He drove a little further ahead and pulled into an unpaved track leading into the forest surrounding Blacke's compound.

From here, he quickly prepared himself, leaving his clothes in the trunk of his car. Going in full bear would allow him a certain amount of stealth he could not muster in his human form. Within seconds, he was ready to shift.

Henry trudged through the forest, heading straight for the boundary fence. He closed his eyes and focused. Although Gail must have been at least a few hundred yards away from him, he could catch her scent already.

A few large trees near the fence allowed him to cross easily. From there, it was just a matter of following his nose. It didn't take long for him to find her.

You made it, Henry thought.

She held up a Tupperware box. *Lunch break, remember? So. Let's talk.*

Henry nodded. *We're the same, you and I. These new initiatives Black wants to implement... He needs to be stopped.*

Yes. Gail wrapped her arms around herself.

I feel like I can trust you.

She raised her head and stared at him. It was unnerving, like she could see through all the bullshit, right to his core. *You* can *trust me.*

I had this idea, to stand up to Blacke. A new movement of people like us. As many fellow Alliance members as we can recruit, and regular people.

Gail cocked her head to the side. *To what end?*

Once we gain sufficient momentum, we go public. We'll blow the lid off the whole secrecy bullshit. We educate the human population, so they know not to fear us. We'll only be free if we can live out in the open.

Are you sure that's wise?

Henry heard Gail's question, but he was pretty certain she wouldn't need much convincing. He could feel her growing excitement spill over into himself. Not only could he hear her thoughts - how, he wasn't quite sure - he could sense her emotions as well now.

Think about it. Right now our people have so much to fear. Not only are the Sons after our blood, it's our own people, our own Alliance people who are surveilling us, to make sure we don't do anything wrong. Henry paused, waiting for Gail's input.

You're right. It's unacceptable.

Again, her words didn't quite match her vibe. It was distracting. As much as she disapproved of Blacke's radical ideas, she seemed... happy? It didn't make a lot of sense.

I can't do this alone, though. I need a partner, Henry thought.

I imagine you do, Gail answered.

Will you help me?

The more he looked at her, the more distracted he could feel himself become. His bear didn't often speak up, but right now, fully shifted, he had no choice but to listen to his primal call. She was beautiful. He wanted her.

Gail smiled and nodded, and Henry had to stop himself from pouncing.

No way, Henry wasn't about to let himself go off track. He'd always tried to be a good person; honest, loyal. He wasn't about to throw all that away. Henry swallowed hard and forced himself to shut down any remaining yearnings for the temptation that stood before him. Maggie would be waiting for him at home. He wouldn't betray her, or his own ideals.

That's all? You want my help? Gail asked, her mood wavering suddenly.

What a strange question. Henry observed her for a moment. Her eyes still tried to bore a hole in him.

It's not going to be easy, but it's the right way forward, he thought.

She nodded, then looked away. A strange melancholy seemed to overwhelm Gail and him along with her. They'd agreed to work together; wasn't that a good thing? Then why did she exude all this sadness? And why did it tear at him so much? He had to fix it, but he didn't know how.

You're the only one I have confided in, Henry thought.

Gail took a deep breath and looked away roughly in the direction of where Henry knew the Alliance building was located. *I should probably get back. How and when do we do this?* she asked.

We can meet at a farmhouse not too far from here. We'll be safe there.

Gail nodded. *Give me your number.*

They exchanged numbers and another awkward glance, before Gail turned to leave.

What a strange conversation they'd had, without even exchanging a single word out loud. And what an unusual, intriguing woman Gail was.

Henry had never had the benefit of reading anyone's mind, especially not a woman's mind. He had no idea what went on in Maggie's head most of the time.

Was she this complex as well? As guided by emotion?

Perhaps, though deep inside he suspected Gail *was* different. Either way, it didn't matter. Considering their unique connection, they'd work well together.

Henry returned to his car and changed back into his human self, making sure as before that he wasn't overlooked. From there he drove off straight to the farmhouse he'd alluded to; his childhood home.

Scottish Werebear: A Painful Dilemma

He'd send Gail the directions upon arriving and wait for her to drop in after work. That's when they'd begin.

CHAPTER SIX

When Gail got back to her desk, she was still reeling with conflicted emotions. The encounter with Henry Weston had left her confused.

He obviously sensed her much more keenly now; that's what had allowed them to communicate so easily. And she'd felt whatever he'd felt. The attraction, the pull they seemed to have between them. She'd been ecstatic at first, sharing a secret meeting in the woods, just the two of them.

But he'd rejected their shared desires - he'd rejected *her*. Like none of what they shared meant anything. He wanted a partner to start some kind of revolution. He didn't want anything more intimate than that.

And who was this Maggie he'd kept thinking about?

Gail dropped the still full lunchbox into a drawer underneath her desk and pulled up files on the Glasgow office - the same ones she'd consulted earlier in the day in an effort to find out more about Henry himself. *Maggie, Maggie, Maggie.*

It didn't take her long to find a dossier about a Margaret who worked in Henry's office. So that was her.

Gail squinted at the picture that accompanied the file. She was a fierce looking brunette, reasonably attractive, fit.

So they were an item? Henry and her? The thought made Gail ill.

It was not supposed to be this way. When you find your mate, that was supposed to be it. There wasn't supposed to be any hesitation, any doubt. You were supposed to just follow your instincts and pair up.

Only Henry didn't seem to want to do that. All because of this woman.

Gail bit her bottom lip and fought the tears stinging in

her eyes. This had been only the third time she'd met him, but somehow he'd made a space for himself in her heart. She should have told him to go away, that she wanted nothing to do with his revolutionary plans if he didn't also accept her as his mate. All or nothing.

She hadn't said anything of the sort, of course. Because she couldn't face the thought of *what if.* What if he'd rejected her demand? What if she never saw him again?

No, as much as it hurt, she had to meet with him again. She would do as asked and help him with his new movement. It helped that she shared his ideologies, so working together shouldn't be too difficult.

But it would hurt, being around him without being able to act on her instincts.

And he *had* felt something too, dammit! She had felt his lust as if it were her own.

This was *not* how these things were supposed to go!

"Hello, Love," a familiar voice behind Gail made her feel even more queasy.

"Agent Dumbarton, how can I help?" Gail pressed her lips together as she turned to look him in the eye. Instead of Finch, why couldn't Blacke have taken Dumbarton along with him to London? At least that would have gotten him out of her hair.

"Oh, I can think of a few ways." He winked at her.

Ugh. The sight of him made the hairs on the back of her neck stand up. Who the hell did he think he was? This was the wrong time to get on her bad side.

"I don't appreciate your tone," Gail snapped.

"Oh, don't you?" Dumbarton leaned down, resting his huge palm on the desk beside her, blocking her in.

Everything down to his scent repulsed her. Gail felt her skin tingle, the first sign that her inner bear was readying for a fight. Blacke was fond of Dumbarton, after all, they shared a similar propensity for violence, so getting into a physical altercation with him would not go down well. But Gail was close to not caring anymore about what her boss thought.

If it came down to it, she would defend herself against this brute.

"Well, perhaps you can relay a message to the boss."

"Sure," Gail said.

Breathe in, breathe out. Calm down.

"You can tell him that the prototypes for Project Safeguard are ready for field testing."

Gail nodded and made a show of noting down Dumbarton's message.

"Anything else?" she barked.

"No, darling. That's all for now." Dumbarton grinned at her and retreated from her desk.

Gail continued to stare at him as he took a couple of steps back and finally left her office. That's when she breathed a sigh of relief. God, how much she hated that guy.

———— ◆ ————

It was shortly after five o'clock when Gail started packing up her things, ready to leave. She'd received the message with Henry's directions a few hours earlier and memorized them. He'd asked her to leave her phone behind at the office, just in case Blacke had installed some kind of tracking software.

It was a bit paranoid, that request, but then again, tracking his own staff seemed like something Blacke would be capable of.

As she left the building, bracing herself against the frosty air, her nerves kicked in. What if she wouldn't be able to do this? Stay professional when every fiber in her body tried its best to do the opposite?

Well, tough. If she couldn't cope, that would be his problem. He would have sensed how she felt and asked for her help anyway. And *he* was the one trying to deny nature. It was all on him.

She navigated through the narrow roads leading away from the Alliance HQ, but rather than head home, she drove in the opposite direction. Gail had no trouble finding her way. Not only had she studied the route carefully all afternoon, it seemed like her instincts were guiding her right to Henry's position.

Of course, they did, he was her mate after all. Not that he accepted that.

Gail wrapped her fingers tighter around the steering until her knuckles turned white. This was going to be difficult.

By the time she pulled into the long driveway leading to the farm Henry had described in his message, she felt like she could pinpoint his exact location on the compound. He was waiting for her inside, heading for the front door.

The door opened just as she expected it to; only it wasn't just Henry greeting her. There was an elderly lady with him as well.

Gail got out and nodded at Henry, who immediately introduced her.

"Gail McPherson. A colleague from the Alliance." Henry's deep baritone made Gail's heart skip a few beats.

Gail offered her hand to the woman, who just stood there, smiling subtly first at her, then at Henry.

"A colleague. Sure, son. Whatever you say." Finally, she did shake Gail's hand. "Helen Weston."

Henry looked at her, one eyebrow raised. Clearly this introduction hadn't gone quite how he had wanted it to.

"Nice to meet you, Mrs. Weston," Gail mumbled.

"No need to be so formal, sweetheart. Just call me Helen."

Gail nodded, though couldn't quite bring herself to do as asked.

Meanwhile, Henry was restlessly shifting his weight from one foot to the other. "Let's begin, shall we?"

"Sure," Gail agreed and followed him inside the house.

Henry led the way up the stairs, past framed old

photographs and other mementos. When he had instructed her to come here, Gail never expected to actually be invited into the house he'd grown up in.

She took it all in. There were some pictures of just Henry when he was a boy, some with a man who bore a significant resemblance to him - probably his dad. Then there were the inevitable, much more formal family portraits of the three of them including his mother.

All of the photographs were decades old.

Unfortunately, Henry's pace didn't allow Gail to study each one of them carefully; she only managed a cursory glance while walking up the stairs and down the corridor, arriving at last in what must be the study. Shelves of dusty books lined the room, a grouping of leather arm chairs in the corner. There was a desk as well, shoehorned in between boxes upon boxes of old papers.

It was messy, but Gail felt comfortable at once. It looked a lot like Dad's study did, or at least how it used to look back before his retirement.

"We can work here," Henry said.

Gail nodded and stole a glance at him. So handsome. So tempting... While she admired him, he barely even looked up or paid attention to her.

Stop it, she reprimanded herself. If he wasn't interested in her, why should she be? The best thing for both of them would be to just get on with the job they'd come here for. Do the work and go home.

Henry sighed deeply as he sat down in one of the padded wooden chairs surrounding the desk and rubbed his forehead. Was he struggling with this as well?

"I have a mate already," Henry spoke softly, but his words were ringing in Gail's ears nevertheless.

"I know," she responded.

"As awkward as it is, I don't know who to trust with this." He gestured around at the boxes.

A closer look revealed they had Alliance labels on them. Had he taken home old records? What for?

"I understand," Gail forced herself to reply. *How about your so-called mate? Can't you trust her with this instead?*

Henry shook his head. "It's complicated."

Gail sat down opposite him and rested her bag against one of the legs of the desk. It wasn't any of her business why he wasn't working on all this with Maggie. What did she care?

Fine, whatever. Let's get to work.

And work, they did. After that initial ice-breaker, it surprisingly became easier to stay on task too. They understood each other perfectly. They agreed on a great deal of things, and their skills and experience complemented each other well too.

Henry knew how to do field work; Gail knew how Blacke ran his office and had access to information Henry could have never obtained.

Before they knew it, they'd spent hours in that little room, discussing strategy, drawing up plans and studying some of the files Henry had obtained. Dinner, which his mom had lovingly prepared, had been their only interruption.

Suddenly, by late evening, they'd gone from a whole lot of wishful thinking regarding how things *should be* to having a workable plan on how to make it happen. The New Alliance was born.

It was already past midnight when they said their goodbyes. Despite the initial difficulties, Gail felt a lot more positive about what she had come here to do. If she couldn't have him as a mate, at least they'd become friends.

Gail drove home largely on autopilot.

As much as it pained her to admit it to herself, he was right to want to remain faithful to Maggie. Henry wasn't the sort of man to shy away from his commitments. He was honorable and faithful. If only he had been hers.

CHAPTER SEVEN

When Henry got home that night, Maggie was already asleep. He took care to make as little noise as possible getting ready for bed.

Today had been a giant leap in the right direction. With Gail's help, this new movement of theirs actually had a chance.

The one thing he couldn't get out of his head, though, was how she'd made him feel. He'd tried to let her down easy - a near impossible feat, considering he couldn't even look at her straight. The hurt he knew she felt at his rejection had just made things harder.

Now, as he stood beside the bed in their shared apartment, he couldn't look at Maggie straight either. Something felt wrong.

It's because I'm lying to her. Hiding what I'm up to, Henry tried to convince himself. That didn't seem right, though. More likely, he was guilty because he'd put himself in a position where he was going to spend a significant amount of time with another woman. One he found difficult to resist.

And what was worse, no matter how hard he'd fought it, he'd started to care for the other woman as well.

She's just a colleague. We're only working together, nothing else.

He'd tried repeating those words in his head all evening, and they still didn't ring quite true.

But what was he to do? If he wanted the New Alliance to be successful, he'd need the help. It wasn't easy to find someone who believed in the same things. He would have never even found out about Gail's ideologies if he hadn't heard her voice in his head. Surely that meant that her involvement was somehow meant to be?

Henry carefully got into bed and closed his eyes but

couldn't find rest. Images of Gail danced in front of his mind's eye, forcing him to open his eyes again to stare at the ceiling.

They'd had their ups and downs, Maggie and him. But never before had he felt so alone in her company.

———◆———

The next morning, Henry started to put one of his plans into action. He drafted in the whole Glasgow office. Everyone was to investigate certain high-risk individuals in an effort to identify anyone engaging in so-called *unacceptable behavior.*

They had identified so many potential suspects that he broke procedure and ordered his agents into the field individually rather than in pairs. His reasons for this were two-fold: he'd have the opportunity to sneak away to the farm without Maggie noticing, and his agents would be forced to observe rather than act if they found anything untoward.

It was one thing arresting someone when it was two-against-one, but to confront a riled up bear who might think his mate's safety was being threatened? Nobody on his team would be reckless enough to attempt it, not even Maggie.

Blacke's orders, Henry had said. *Forget about the Sons; we've handed them off to HQ. I expect results on this. Find me some rule-breakers and fast.*

As the office started to clear out, with all his agents leaving to start their individual assignments, he was left behind at his desk. It was shocking how easily everyone had accepted their orders. As if nobody saw the insanity in violating the privacy of their own people on such a large scale.

Henry listlessly stared at the papers on his desk; he was unable to focus on any words in particular, though. It was all just a blur.

He sat back and rubbed his eyes. Thanks to his late return from the farm, he'd not had much sleep. If there was one thing bears didn't like, it was a lack of sleep or food for that matter.

But this was not the time for rest. A strong and extra sweet cup of coffee later, Henry forced himself back to work. After handing off the field jobs to his team, it was down to him to contact all the shifter families with young children to inform them about the tracker project. It wasn't ideal, trying to gauge their reactions over the phone, but this was the only way he could do it by himself.

Then, by the afternoon, he'd make a quick call to Gail to update her with any progress made. In turn, she would give him the latest updates on what was happening at the HQ.

That's exactly how the day went, and the day after that. By the third day into this new routine, some of Henry's team, most notably Maggie, had gathered actionable intel.

They were starting to deliver Henry's so-called rule-breakers, just as he had ordered. File after file containing observations from his agents landed on his desk. It was down to him to decide follow-up action.

It was sickening. All these lives, which Blacke intended to ruin. Couples, even families, to be torn apart. And everyone except Henry was so enthusiastic about it too.

At the same time, his work on Project Safeguard was chugging along slowly. He'd made progress for Blacke - a lot of the families sounded positive. Fear was a strong motivator to throw one's privacy out the window. This was bad news for the New Alliance.

"Another one?" Henry asked, his heart heavy with dread as Maggie delivered yet another file.

"This one's the most promising one yet. The couple has been together for years." She grinned at him.

"And the man is human, you say?" Henry asked, scanning Maggie's report.

"Yep. I verified it myself."

"Good job," Henry mumbled while flipping the page to find some holiday snaps of the couple together.

"So, when do we go in?" Maggie asked.

"This is a delicate matter. We don't want to tip off the others, or they might try to run," Henry reasoned. Actually, he didn't want to take official action at all, just approach these people himself to drum up support for the New Alliance.

"Understood. So... When?"

"I'll discuss it with Headquarters. Perhaps they've drawn up some guidelines..."

Maggie squinted at him and pursed her lips. What was she thinking? How convenient it would be if he could just read her thoughts too.

"In the meantime, here are some more cases you can look into." Henry handed her a stack of new files. "Good work. Keep it up."

She didn't look pleased, but he couldn't afford to get into a lengthy conversation about it right now either. Henry picked up another pending file off his desk and pretended to read until she walked away.

He counted the reports his agents had turned in. Half a dozen already, with more to come as they completed their various assignments. He'd contact HQ today, but not to ask for Blacke's orders on the matter.

After visiting with these people, he'd have to let Gail know about their progress.

Once Maggie had left the premises again, he picked up the first file from his desk. The one she'd just delivered. *Most promising indeed...* These people would have the most to lose.

Henry would start with them, try to reason with the woman on her own first, then perhaps involve the human partner in discussions as well.

It took him the whole afternoon to track them down, but at last, he managed to locate the woman, Irene Finch, and take her aside for a quiet chat outside her office.

"What is it you want from me, exactly?" she asked while studying his ID.

"Well - I hope you don't mind me calling you Irene-" Henry began.

She shook her head.

"You know about what we do at the Alliance?"

"Yeah. You investigate threats against shifters."

"Right, well, let's say that in recent times the Alliance's focus has shifted - excuse the pun."

"I don't understand." Irene gave Henry back his credentials.

"You might want to sit down." Henry nodded at a park bench near where they were standing.

She reluctantly followed him and took a seat. That's when he told her the whole Alliance story, from beginning to end. About Blacke's new initiatives, the trackers, the concerns about secrecy.

By the end, Irene had turned white as a sheet.

"What do we do? Clive is my mate. I can't just-" She held her head in her hands. "Oh, God."

"It's okay. I don't agree with them either. A few of us are planning an initiative of our own."

"I'm listening."

And so Henry told her a better-rehearsed version of what he'd said to Matt that day. Going public was the only way forward. If he didn't already believe in his cause so strongly, he would have convinced himself. Luckily, Irene agreed.

She was in. And even better, she knew a whole bunch of couples not yet on the Alliance radar who were in a very similar situation. With her help, the New Alliance would grow significantly overnight.

They called it viral marketing; Henry had read up on it. When you tell your friends about something, and they tell their friends. Within a short time, the number of people involved would grow exponentially, just like a virus.

By the time he left Irene, Henry was feeling pumped. It

would soon get dark, early as it always did in winter. But he wasn't ready to head back to the office. Instead, he informed Gail of his progress and then pulled out the next file from the stack his agents had turned in. Perhaps he'd be able to locate another potential recruit.

They had no time to lose. Sooner or later, Maggie would lose patience and insist that they start rounding people up. He could only protect these couples for so long.

———◆———

By the time Henry got home, Maggie was already sitting in her usual seat at the dinner table, waiting. It had been her turn to cook tonight; food was on the table.

"Where have you been?" she asked.

He waved away her question. "Oh, I was just talking to some of the families who are good candidates for Project Safeguard. Some needed a bit more convincing than what I could manage over the phone." He took off his coat and eagerly joined her. "This smells amazing."

Henry smiled at her, but she didn't reciprocate.

"Potatoes?" Maggie held up the dish in his direction.

"Thanks."

The food tasted good too. Running around all afternoon had made him hungry, so he didn't hesitate to load up his plate. As he started to eat, Maggie just observed him.

"So how many candidates have we got?" she asked finally.

He shrugged. "Most of my afternoon was spent just trying to convince one set of parents. Don't you miss the good old days, when our days were spent running after the bad guys?" Henry joked.

Maggie didn't crack even the smallest of smiles. "We're still doing that, running after bad guys, just more quietly."

"Right," Henry said. Spying on unsuspecting people

who might have mistakenly fallen in love with the wrong person would have been a more accurate description.

"I feel like I hardly see you anymore, now that we're working apart every day," Maggie remarked.

Henry looked up, to find those sharp eyes of hers staring at him.

"Perhaps we can go away somewhere, just the two of us, this weekend?" she suggested.

Henry looked down at his plate again and loaded his fork with more meat.

"Actually, I was hoping to visit mom again. As you know, she's-"

"I know," Maggie interrupted him. "She's been having a hard time lately."

She picked up her half-full plate and put some of the potatoes back into the dish. Then she got up and carried it towards the kitchen.

"You're done?" Henry asked.

Maggie didn't respond.

Henry shrugged and continued eating. They'd had some version of this argument already the day before he'd driven up to Stirling to meet Gail. Why Maggie seemed so jealous of him spending time with his mother, he'd never understand. He never did understand what went on inside her head most of the time.

Once finished, he did his half of the work for the evening; tidying up the kitchen. Then, he wanted nothing more than to crash for the night.

Maggie was already asleep on her side of the bed, so he took care not to make too much noise.

As soon as he'd rested his head on the pillow, just a couple of little words turned his world up-side-down.

"Who's Gail?"

CHAPTER EIGHT

Ever since Blacke had returned from his short visit to London, Gail's days had become busier than ever. There was always someone to call, a memo to write, a parcel to courier.

At the same time, her nights were shorter than ever. When she wasn't coordinating with Henry over the phone, she spent a ridiculous amount of time fantasizing about him. It was painful, recalling the details of their few meetings, and yet she couldn't stop thinking about him.

This morning was no different. Gail had been drifting in and out of sleep for hours; her mind occupied with just one thing. Every time she'd closed her eyes, the same images had overwhelmed her. Henry, looking at her with the love and admiration she knew he'd be capable of, if only he'd accept that fate intended for them to be together.

If she let herself, the images would get more intimate, more intense.

Oh, why not. She'd never felt anything as exciting as what she experienced when she let her mind run wild with the fantasy of Henry Weston.

All the bears she knew had hard, strong bodies, but none of them had anything on Henry. The visions her imagination chose to feed her were beyond compare. He was perfect.

Henry hovered over her for a moment, holding his weight up with those muscular arms of his. His eyes focused on her lips for a moment, then he dove down and tasted her.

Gail sighed. It never took long for the fantasy to have an effect.

She reached down between her legs and felt that she was already wet.

He lowered himself on top of her, slowly. His naked skin felt hot against her fingertips as she explored the contours of his upper arms and back. Gail reached around him and pulled him against her tighter.

Together, they made the perfect couple. Hard muscle against soft curves.

Gail had never dated much. A true romantic, she'd held out for Mr. Right. The one upside to this relative inexperience was that she knew exactly how to take matters into her own hands. Literally.

She writhed against the sheets as her fingertips found those special, forbidden places that very few had found before. What else could she do? This was the best she could hope for. To finger herself to orgasm to the dream of Henry Weston.

There was no way she'd get over him. No way could she bring herself to consider another man.

Gail's moment of ecstasy was short-lived. Her alarm pierced the silence of her bedroom, jerking her back into reality. Damn.

Another day of rushing around the Alliance HQ, running various errands for Blacke, awaited. Despite the pleasure she'd just felt, the loss that overwhelmed her now, while dragging herself out of bed, cut deep. Would she ever experience anything like what she'd fantasized about?

Probably not.

As much as that knowledge hurt, a light still awaited Gail at the end of what was going to be a long, dark day. Her daily phone conversation with Henry. Despite everything, she couldn't wait to hear his voice.

———— ◆ ————

Today, Gail didn't need to wait too long to hear from Henry. By four, he'd sent her a message, giving her some very good news indeed. He'd confronted the first of a number of mixed couples his office had identified in response to Blacke's recent orders.

The woman, Irene Finch, had pledged her support.

Gail smiled and put her phone back into her pocket and picked up the pot of coffee.

"Darling, how about you pour me a cuppa as well?"

Gail closed her eyes and took a deep breath. Don't engage him. Don't encourage him.

"Agent Dumbarton. I'm sure you're capable enough to know your way around a coffee maker." Gail turned to walk off with her boss's mug of coffee. Blond, four sugars, she'd counted them carefully to avoid a repeat of her first week, when she accidentally had added too much.

"Come on! No need to be rude." Dumbarton blocked her way.

"I'm needed in my office," Gail said.

Ugh. What a repugnant man. She didn't have time for this. Gail stepped aside to dodge him to be on her way.

That's when Dumbarton changed position, cutting off her exit route.

"What's the rush, darling?" He grinned.

Her heart started to beat faster, and a thin layer of sweat formed over her entire body. This was unacceptable. His behavior-

Gail scanned the room. Where *was* everybody? Normally, there were at least half a dozen agents hanging around the coffee maker or the water cooler, depending on the season. Another two or three would be sitting at their desks doing actual work.

Today, everyone seemed to have vanished.

Wouldn't someone - anyone - walk in to diffuse this bind Dumbarton had gotten her into?

"Mr. Blacke likes his coffee hot. I don't think-"

"I like something else hot," Dumbarton whispered.

"This is inappropriate," Gail insisted.

"Come on; nobody's around. You don't have to pretend. I know you're well up for it; I can smell it on ya." Dumbarton leaned forward, his face only an inch away from hers and inhaled sharply.

Gail's fight or flight instinct was kicking in. He was bigger and much stronger than her; Dumbarton was another brown bear. If she fought him, he'd win. She'd have to be smarter than that...

So instead of charging forward, she retreated, hitting into the cabinet behind her. She put the mug down - Blacke would not be amused if Gail broke his monogrammed mug - and flung her arm around while diving off to the side as though she'd lost her balance.

She hit her hand into the coffee maker, causing it to crash to the floor beside them.

It made an almighty racket as the glass receptacle smashed into a million pieces. That, plus the flood of hot liquid spilling onto the floor was enough to distract Dumbarton.

"Oh, damn, I'm so clumsy," Gail said. "I'd better get Gerry to clean that up before someone gets hurt."

Dumbarton still stood there, dumbfounded at what had just occurred as she marched off. Gail just remembered to snatch Blacke's still steaming mug from the cabinet before fleeing out the door.

That was a close call.

She looked down at the coffee stains on her suede pumps. Damnit. She really liked these shoes too. Gail rushed into Blacke's office, placing the mug on his desk and immediately retreated to her own desk, right outside. What a relief.

From now on, she'd have to be more vigilant and not allow herself to get cornered by that man again. This, along with all the other crap she'd had to deal with in this job would have been enough to make her quit, if it wasn't for her alternate agenda.

If the New Alliance movement was going to succeed, they needed an insider in Blacke's administration. There was no way she'd give up now that they were getting so close.

"McPherson."

Gail looked up to find Agent Finch standing in the doorway.

"Agent Finch. How can I help?"

He looked around the hallway once before entering her office.

"This is a bit delicate," he started.

Gail observed the man. They hadn't interacted much during her short time working here. The most they'd ever spoken was when she'd made the arrangements for him to travel with Blacke to London. He'd always come across like a quiet man, serious about his work, but without the violent streak some of the others in the office demonstrated.

"Yes?" Gail asked.

Finch gestured at her to come closer and again checked left and right, probably to make sure they weren't being overheard.

Gail got up and joined him outside, then closed the door. Bears had exceptional hearing, but there was no way Blacke would be able to hear them with this kind of distance and a closed door between them.

"Well handled, the matter with Dumbarton," Finch said.

Gail took a step backward, hitting into the door from behind. "You saw that?"

"Not the whole thing. I was about to intervene when you- Well, good job."

"Was that all you wanted to tell me?" Gail frowned. This was an awkward conversation to have. Some things were best left undiscussed.

"Actually, I do have this." Agent Finch handed her the dossier he'd been holding. "I trust you'll know what to do with this."

He looked back and forth again and walked off as if their conversation had never happened.

Weird guy. He seemed awfully paranoid for some reason.

Gail opened the file and read the first sheet. It was a surveillance recommendation that had come in from the Glasgow office.

Her throat went dry when she read the whole thing.

Target Name: Helen Weston.
Requested Mode: Phone tap.

The request had been signed by the most unlikely of people: Henry Weston himself.

Gail closed the file and rushed back inside to her desk. She opened her drawer and found some old reports he'd filed with HQ. The signature was similar enough to convince most people, but not Gail.

There was no way he'd sign anything like that, so who could have done it? The other agents in his office would have access to his signature, so any of them could have faked it. This was bad. Someone within Henry's team had gone rogue.

She had to notify him as soon as possible. Gail checked her watch. It was almost five o'clock. He usually called around six, so she still had a little time to gather more details. Finch had handed her the file, rather than Blacke himself. Did that mean he doubted its authenticity as well?

Had someone else seen it and actually acted on it before it ended up with her?

Gail powered up her computer and checked the inventory. If someone had tapped the phone at Helen Weston's home, they would have had to check out a transmitter. Currently, this was not the case.

"Gail?" Blacke's voice called out from his office.

Gail quickly closed the inventory file and switched off her monitor. "Yes, sir?"

"A word, before you leave."

Typical. There were always a few things Blacke would remember at the end of the day, delaying her journey home. Gail forced a smile as she entered his office.

"I had a thought regarding old man Campbell, downstairs. Note all this down."

Gail nodded and started writing.

"He has a daughter." Blacke folded his hands and sat back with a smug grin on his face. "If we manage to track her down, I wonder if we'll have more luck interrogating him..."

"Very good, Sir. Shall I notify the Edinburgh office?" Gail asked.

Blacke shook his head. "No, I think I'd prefer to have my own men handle this."

CHAPTER NINE

Henry stared at the ceiling. Shit, had Maggie actually just said those words?

"Who's Gail?" she repeated herself.

This was bad.

"You mean Gail McPherson? Blacke's personal assistant," he responded, in as calm a voice as he could manage.

"Aha..." Maggie said.

Was that it? Was that all she wanted to know?

"Why do you ask?" Henry asked though he wasn't certain he wanted to know exactly. What on earth had he done to spark this question?

"Is there any particular reason why she would call you after hours?"

Call him? What was she talking about? Henry instinctively reached for the spot on the bedside table where he always kept his phone, but there was nothing there.

"You'd left it in your coat." Maggie tossed the mobile onto his side of the bed. It landed in the center of Henry's chest.

He had a quick look. Three missed calls, the earliest at six in the evening.

"She must have been responding to the message I left, about how to proceed with those couples. Like I told you this morning, remember?" Henry explained, his mind racing. Had Gail sent any messages as well? Had Maggie *read* them? He generally made sure to delete his conversations with Gail; had he accidentally left something behind for Maggie to find?

Hang on, why was he feeling guilty? He wasn't doing anything wrong. They were just working together, Gail and him. Why was he making excuses and behaving like he'd cheated somehow?

"I can't do this anymore," Maggie whispered.

Wait, what?!

Henry sat up straight and turned to face Maggie.

"You can't do *what* anymore? What do you think is going on here exactly?"

Maggie shrugged. "Ever since the other week, when you drove down to Gartcosh by yourself - if that's where you actually went... I feel like we might as well live on two different planets, you and I. And don't try to deny it. You're not the same person." Her tone was ambiguous. Henry couldn't make out if she was angry, sad, or just fishing for a reaction.

Henry wanted to protest but decided to hold out. Perhaps she was just venting her frustrations about his refusal to take her away for the weekend.

"I saw you look at her, when Blacke was at the office. I didn't think much of it at the time, but now things are falling into place."

"There's nothing going on between Gail and me."

"So you call her *Gail*. That's how well you know each other!" Maggie taunted.

Damn. He'd walked right into that one.

"We've been talking a lot about Project Safeguard lately. Yeah, I know her a little bit."

Maggie nodded but refused to make eye contact with him or even turn in his direction. She just remained as she was, on her back, staring straight at the ceiling.

Things weren't so uncertain anymore. She was definitely angry and trying to cover it up.

Henry rested his hand on her arm, only for her to shake it off.

"Just come right out with it. Beating around the bush doesn't suit you," Henry said.

That's when he got a reaction. She turned her head and shot him a deadly glare. Maggie was not amused at all.

"Fine. Have it your way. Have you been *fucking* Gail McPherson? Huh?" she didn't speak the words as much as spat them out and folded her arms. Her eyes were once more glued to the ceiling.

"No." Henry shook his head, then leaned over to get back into Maggie's line of sight. "No! Look at me. I haven't touched the woman. Like I said, we've just been working together."

"Working together. That's just great." Maggie let out a fake chuckle. "I wasn't born yesterday. Does Blacke know the two of you are *working together*? And I don't know her, but who the hell makes work calls at nine in the fucking evening? Nobody is that dedicated, not even Blacke's precious little personal assistant."

"Look, Maggie, darling..." Henry tried to touch her again, but she flinched like the first time.

"I don't want to hear it."

"And Tuesday night? When you came home who knows when? You were with her, weren't you?"

So far, Henry had been skirting around the truth but not actually lied about Gail. Of course, he hadn't done anything appropriate. Not that he hadn't wanted to with every cell in his body. It would be easier to deny it, but that wasn't his style.

"Yes. Although I went to the farm that day, I was near Stirling anyway, so I felt it wise to arrange for a meeting."

"At night?"

"In the evening. It ran late."

"I don't want to talk about this anymore," Maggie's voice sounded choked with anger. "I think it would be best if you left now."

"What? This is my home too!" Henry protested.

"Just believe me. It's best for both of us. Just leave." Maggie turned onto her side facing away from Henry.

He was generally a patient guy, at least he liked to think so. And fair, he was fair as well. And despite his attraction for Gail, he hadn't crossed the line with her. Maggie had no right to kick him out of the house!

At the same time, if he wanted to increase his chances of making things right with her, perhaps it would be better to do as he was told. He'd give her this little victory, with a view to picking up this conflict later, and winning the war, as it were.

He'd explain everything, demonstrate how much Maggie meant to him, and things would work themselves out.

Henry got out of bed, put on the same clothes he'd changed out of only a little while earlier, and threw a few random items into a backpack. He was going to leave, if that's what Maggie wanted. But not empty-handed.

Once the bag was full, and he'd retrieved his toothbrush and other necessities from the bathroom, he left. He didn't say goodbye or look back. That would have just made Maggie's anger flare back up again.

There was nowhere for him to go, except one place. It wouldn't be comfortable, but at least the holding cells were empty ever since he'd delivered those prisoners to HQ the previous week. Tonight, it would be just him in that building.

Things would look different come morning.

Henry hadn't had a good night. Throughout, if there wasn't a strange rustle or creak somewhere in the building disturbing his sleep, there were those incessant dreams he couldn't get rid of. Gail.

It was infuriating.

This. This right here was the reason Maggie had thrown him out. And as much as he fought Gail's pull on him, he just couldn't shut it off completely.

And the worst part was, he still had no idea how to make things right with Maggie. It was all his own fault, wasn't it? There was no excuse, no justification that would pacify her. *The truth.*

The truth would piss her off in an entirely new way. They'd made progress, Gail and him, but they were far from ready to go public with their plan. She'd never be convinced right now, would she?

But it was all he had.

Henry got up at five, stretching his aching limbs on his way out of the holding cell he'd repurposed as a bedroom for the night. The hard cots the Alliance had provided were far from comfortable, especially for someone as tall as Henry.

Once at his desk, coffee in hand, he let his mind run through the various potential outcomes for Maggie and him. He had no other choice. Maggie needed to know the truth.

So he waited. And waited some more.

By eight, the first agents started to arrive. Some looked surprised to find Henry already at work, but nobody said anything.

Maggie was nowhere to be seen, though.

Finally, by nine-thirty, Henry had had enough. It was one thing to turn him out of his own home after accusing him of stuff he didn't actually do. But she had a job to do here. Not showing up for it was unprofessional and very unlike her. So he did what he would have, had any other team member not shown up for work; he called her. No answer.

That was it. If she wasn't going to come in on her own accord, he'd have to go to her.

"Maggie, open up!" Henry called out through the letterbox of what had been their shared apartment for the past two years. He'd tried unlocking it, but Maggie must have put the latch on from the inside.

There was some movement inside but no response.

He knocked on the door again, harder this time.

No way would he just give up on this. Their relationship meant too much to him.

"I'll explain everything. Believe me, you will want to hear this," Henry pleaded.

He waited around a little longer, listening for Maggie's footsteps inside. Finally, he heard her approach.

The lock clicked, and the door opened just a crack.

"Not here. I don't want to discuss Alliance business out in the street," Henry said.

Maggie pressed her lips together in contempt and averted her gaze to the floor. Then she stepped aside, allowing Henry inside the house.

"Make it quick," Maggie said and folded her arms. Like the previous night, she didn't even look at him.

"I left last night to give you space. But I never did anything with that woman. Please believe me," Henry whispered.

Did she not know him at all? How could she think he'd be unfaithful?

"So why was she calling you at nine in the evening? And don't give me the same bullshit again. I can tell when you're lying," Maggie said.

"Then look at me. You'll see I'm telling the truth." Henry reached for her, guiding her chin up toward him.

"It wasn't Alliance business, not exactly. But we are working together."

Maggie cocked her head to the side, frowning. Her eyes were cold; he couldn't read them.

"You remember when we had dinner the other week. I was talking about some doubts I had..."

"What does that have to do with-"

"I'm getting to it. Just let me finish."

Maggie sighed, then looked away again. Somehow, not having her stare him down actually made it easier to explain the rest.

"For a while now, I've felt like we're heading in a

dangerous direction, the Alliance is, I mean. Like our focus has shifted from our actual enemies towards members of our own community who have made certain lifestyle choices..."

"Secrecy is the only way we have to ensure our safety," Maggie argued.

"I'm not sure of that anymore. If we educate the human population- if we show them that they have nothing to fear from us..." Henry said.

"They'll hunt us down. We won't be fighting just a small group of humans, but millions of them!" Maggie took a step back and glared at him.

"People are better than that. They're only afraid of what they don't know. We just have to make sure that we're the ones talking to them, rather than the Sons!" Henry took a step forward, placing his hand on her arm.

Maggie shook her head, slowly at first, then more violently.

"No, I don't accept that. And I can't believe that someone who works in Blacke's very own office would believe that either."

"But she does. Gail does believe that. That's what we've been working on together. To figure out a way to educate people!" Henry said.

"I don't want to hear her name anymore."

"Okay..." Henry squeezed Maggie's arm. At least, she wasn't retreating anymore.

"And I can't accept these crazy ideas of yours." Maggie bit her bottom lip.

"They're not crazy. Just give it a chance, once we get support..."

"No. No way. I can't."

"Please, Mags. This is important to me," Henry pleaded.

She shook her head again. "No. This is it. You have to decide what's more important to you. This stupid plan or our relationship."

Scottish Werebear: A Painful Dilemma

Henry couldn't believe his ears. He could understand that she had trouble seeing his side of things - she could be very stubborn after all. But to make him choose?

"I mean it, Henry. You pick. Me or *this*..." Maggie gestured at him. "This lunacy."

Henry took a deep breath. That was it. He wouldn't give up on Maggie. She was his mate.

So he had to bear another loss. To win the war.

CHAPTER TEN

Gail woke up early. But it wasn't the same old visions of Henry that had roused her from her sleep; it was something else. A nagging feeling in the pit of her stomach. Something was wrong, and she couldn't figure out what it was.

For hours, she tossed and turned, but that feeling never left her. Was she coming down with something? Or perhaps she was dreading going to work because of what had happened with Dumbarton yesterday?

The thought of him just made her angry, not anxious. She'd freed herself of him once; she'd do it again. No, something else was causing this.

Unfortunately, without knowing what it was, Gail couldn't do anything about it. So she followed her usual routine and went to work as if nothing had happened.

By the ten o'clock, she was a nervous wreck. No matter what she tried, she couldn't focus at all. What had started as an awkward sort of sensation in her stomach, had grown and evolved. Palpitations, cold sweats; it was as though she had a fever coming on, but with none of the usual symptoms of the season flu that had been going around.

Finally, she couldn't take it anymore and hid herself away in the ladies' room. The reflection looking back at her from the mirror didn't look like her usual self. Normally, she never had dark circles, but this morning she did. Her skin had turned from its normal warm olive to a sickly sort of yellow even foundation couldn't fix properly.

Gail was still staring at herself wondering what had happened to her overnight when her mobile rang, scaring her half to death.

She fumbled with her handbag and retrieved it as quickly as she could. Henry. Her chest tightened, breaths quickened. That was it. Something was wrong with him!

"Hello?" she answered, her voice trembling noticeably.

"Gail. What I'm about to ask of you isn't fair, I know. But I have no other choice." Henry's voice sounded flat. Gail couldn't detect emotion in his tone at all.

"What's wrong? Something's happened; I could feel it all morning!" she blurted out.

"It's best not to dwell on things. The bottom line is, I can't work with you anymore."

Gail was speechless. That wasn't what she expected him to say at all.

"You don't want my help anymore?" she asked finally.

"No, no. Your help is more crucial than ever. I'm talking about my own involvement. I can't-" Henry took a deep breath. "The New Alliance must go on without me."

Gail turned her back against the wall and sank to the floor. This was it. The terrible black cloud that had been hanging over her. Henry was terminating their working relationship.

Why, though? There was only one reason that made sense. Somehow, Maggie must have found out about it and forced his hand.

"This was your project. Your idea. How will I continue on my own?" Gail whispered. *How will I survive on my own if I never see you again?*

Silent tears streamed down her face.

"It's not my choice. My duty is to my mate first."

So Maggie *was* the one who had inspired his sudden decision. Gail hated her with all her heart. How dare she interfere in the good work they were doing? The New Alliance would ensure the safety of generations of shifters to come.

At the very least, someone had to stop Blacke before he put his latest ideas into practice. The man was trying to secure his position, and it would be near impossible to get rid of him once he succeeded.

"Your duty isn't to your people as well? Isn't that why you took a job with the Alliance in the first place?" Gail argued.

"I'm sorry. I can't do this anymore." With those last words, Henry hung up.

Gail dropped the phone into her lap and rested her head in her hands. She couldn't contain her despair anymore and started to sob, her whole body trembling as she released the heartache she felt.

It was like being cut in half. His duty was to his mate first, bah! That Maggie woman was only his mate in name. Their connection wasn't real, it couldn't be, not after everything Gail had felt in his presence.

He'd already discarded her as a lover from the moment they started working together, but as long as they kept in touch, there had been a glimmer of hope. One day he might see the truth for himself. One day he might understand that they were meant to be.

But now, this? After all she had done for him? The New Alliance wouldn't have been possible without her help; he'd said so himself. And she'd believed in the cause as much as he did. How dare he leave her alone in this! *How dare he!*

Gail wasn't sure how long she'd sat there, waiting for the flow of tears to stop. Blacke would be wondering where she was... Gail got herself up off the cold bathroom floor and looked in the mirror.

In one morning, she'd aged a decade.

This just wasn't right. Why couldn't things just be

simple, like they were supposed to be? They were supposed to be partners, and now she was alone. Gail couldn't begin to think about how she'd handle things.

She bit her lip and took out a wet wipe from her handbag. If she had to go out there and face her boss, she couldn't do it with streaks of mascara on her cheeks.

It took her a while, but by the end, Gail had eliminated most of the evidence of her breakdown. Of course, she couldn't do much about the redness in her eyes or the puffiness...

She picked up her bag and left, keeping her eyes mostly on the polished wooden floor on the way to her office. Blacke never paid much attention to her, just barked orders through the intercom and expected her to quietly act on them. Hopefully, he wouldn't take note of her today either.

"Gail," Blacke's voice made her flinch as she sat down at her desk.

"Yes, Sir?" she answered, with as steady a voice as she could.

"In here, if you please."

Oh, crap. Had she done something wrong?

Gail pushed her chair back and got up again, her calves aching with every step.

Once inside, she folded her hands in front of her and kept her head down and gaze averted.

"Where have you been? I've been calling for you for the better part of an hour!" Blacke demanded. Damn, had she been hiding out for that long?

"I'm sorry, Sir. I was..." Gail sighed. She had nothing.

"If your work here is too demanding, do let me know. There are plenty of others who would jump at the opportunity to work here." Blacke pushed his chair back and folded his arms as he stared in her direction. He'd never looked at her directly for this long before.

"I understand, Sir. It's not that."

"Approach," Blacke ordered.

Gail did as asked.

"Closer."

She took another step towards Blacke's desk, trying her best to remain calm. He wasn't about to pull the same sort of crap she was getting from Dumbarton, was he?

"Are you coming down with something? Be honest," Blacke asked.

Gail finally did look up only to find Blacke frowning at her. He wasn't *concerned* about her wellbeing, was he? That wasn't the Adrian Blacke she had grown accustomed to. She shrugged, not sure how to answer.

"Well, I can't have you infecting anyone here. Not with all the important work we have going on. I think it would be best if you went home."

Blacke picked up a diagram of something or other from his desk and started to focus on that. The conversation was clearly over.

So he had no concern for her after all. He was more worried about coming catching a little cold himself if she stuck around.

If that's what he wanted, Gail wasn't about to argue. She quietly left his office, packed up her things and made a beeline for the exit. After everything that had happened this morning, she needed time to think more than anything. She needed to regroup.

———— ◆ ————

By the evening, Gail had received a number of emails from a generic Yahoo email address. They were unsigned, but she was pretty sure they could only be from Henry. His tone was concise, business-like. The entire thing read more like an Alliance field report than an email.

So this was it, the last time he'd communicate with her.

She fought the tears that tried to force their way out again and instead focused on the information detailed inside the emails. Despite getting out, Henry had compiled all the details she'd need to continue their work. There were names, scans of reports his agents had prepared about various shifters they suspected of illicit activities. A second set of files outlined families who had refused to participate in the tracker program.

Then there was something much more significant: an actual list of people Henry had already approached.

Gail pinched the bridge of her nose and read the list again. The first was Matthew Argyle, unsurprisingly. Along with his name, there was an address, a phone number, and a note in the form of a single word; *reluctant.*

There were a few more names, one of which stood out. Irene Finch. She was the one Henry had approached first. Gail remembered his message about it. Next to her name there was nothing of any use, just an exclamation mark.

The other names on the list did not seem familiar.

A muffled buzz startled Gail. Her phone. She picked up her handbag and looked for it. Maybe it was Henry, making sure she'd received the information.

If that were the case, she ought to not pick up. He couldn't have it both ways; handing the work to her and then continuing his involvement. It was either all or nothing.

The number on the screen wasn't Henry's, though. It was a landline, Glasgow area code.

"Hello?" Gail answered reluctantly.

"Oh. Is this Gail McPherson?" It was a woman, on the other end.

"Yes, who is this?" Gail asked.

"Irene Finch. Agent Weston referred me to you. I want to help. Please let me know what I can do."

Gail sighed and rested her head on her free hand. So that explained the note by her name.

"Very well," Gail responded.

The woman's insistence didn't leave much room for arguments. And anyway, sitting at home feeling sorry for herself wasn't going to do Gail much good.

They agreed to meet that evening, in a quiet country pub just outside the city boundary. The timing wasn't ideal, but the movement had to live on.

When Gail arrived, she was surprised to find the place much fuller than she'd anticipated.

A woman who looked vaguely familiar approached her first.

"You're Gail? Irene. Pleasure to meet you."

Gail reluctantly shook her hand while scanning the room. Over a dozen people stood around the two as they met.

"I've taken the opportunity to invite a few like-minded folks I know." Irene gestured around the crowd. "Bears, humans, wolves; everyone's represented here. And we all feel that the world would be a better place if we all just work together."

Gail smiled. She hadn't wanted to come here tonight while her loss still felt so raw. But now, she was glad that she'd agreed.

CHAPTER ELEVEN

The days following that last phone call to Gail had not been easy for Henry. He'd agreed to stop his involvement with the New Alliance at Maggie's insistence, but that didn't mean he had to be happy about it. In fact, it was like a part of him had died.

The New Alliance had been his idea, his brainchild. It wasn't so much that he wanted credit... He wouldn't be able to see it grow first hand or ensure its success. He couldn't do the one thing he had vowed to always do: work as hard as he could to keep his people safe.

In trying to make Maggie happy, he'd betrayed his conscience. And that had taken its toll.

What was worse, Maggie hadn't been particularly cheerful either. She'd grudgingly let him back into the house, but insisted he sleep in the living room. Every time he left the house for whatever reason, he could feel her suspicious stares boring holes in his back.

And the atmosphere around the office wasn't any better. Perhaps his mind was only playing tricks on him, but sometimes he could swear that his agents were suddenly a lot less eager to take orders from him than in the past.

His capitulation had lost him something significant.

But it was all for the best, to save his relationship with Maggie. She could only be angry with him for so long, right?

During another one of those long, bleak days at the Alliance base, Henry tried his best to stay positive. HQ had been busy, too busy to send an official order for Henry's people to go out and arrest the people they had identified as being involved with someone human. The only thing halfway relevant that he'd received was an unsigned memo

- probably from Gail - specifically instructing every Alliance branch to not just investigate shifters fraternizing with humans, but also those who had chosen to mate outside their own shifter sub-species.

He put the paper down and scratched his chin. What was the point of this? Weren't they all on the same side? How did it matter whether someone got involved with a different shifter? That didn't violate the secrecy rules at all.

"Boss. HQ is on the line," one of his team members, agent Carlisle interrupted.

HQ. That meant Gail.

He wasn't ready for that.

"Take a message. I'm not in," Henry picked up his coat as well as the offending memo and stormed out.

What the hell was he doing? Was he actually running from the woman?

Pathetic.

He paused, but then followed through on his original plan and left the office. No matter how he felt about everything, he was pretty sure Maggie wouldn't take kindly to him chatting with Gail over the phone even if it was official business for a change. Of course, he couldn't avoid her forever, but for now, it was a necessary precaution.

Henry wasn't quite sure where he was going, so he just got into his car and drove off. After navigating the streets around the Alliance office aimlessly for a few minutes, he found himself heading towards the motorway. He only stayed on for a few miles before taking an exit.

His muscles were painfully tight, and he could feel himself get more riled up with every breath. He needed fresh air, space. Preferably without onlookers. He needed to be alone, in order to be himself.

Had Maggie done the same when she'd suspected him of cheating on her? Had she run off into the wild to let her animal side out?

For some reason, his instincts had brought him to Gartcosh, the small suburban settlement where Matthew

Argyle lived. But Henry wasn't headed to his house. Instead, he bypassed the town and headed straight to the neighboring nature reserve.

Henry pulled into the first available parking space he could find near one of the entrances to the reserve. He didn't waste any time, grabbing his phone from the center console and almost jogging into the park. It was raining, and he was the only one crazy enough to go for a nature walk in this weather.

He was about to strip and hide his belonging in the undergrowth when his mobile rang. *God, now what?*

Henry half expected it to be Maggie checking up on where he was, but it wasn't her name on the screen. Gail.

Oh hell no.

He disconnected the call. It had been difficult enough to cut all ties with her last week. He would not get into a rematch with her.

Henry shoved his phone back into the pocket of his jeans and did what he had come here for: go for a run to blow off steam.

———◆———

By the time Henry got back to the office, he'd had three further missed calls from Gail. This was unacceptable. Didn't she realize she was jeopardizing everything? If he spoke to her and Maggie found out about it, she wouldn't take it lightly. What if she turned Gail into Blacke and his goons? The entire movement could go down because of stupid behavior like this.

Henry switched off his phone and removed the battery, stashing everything in his desk drawer. Now he could breathe easier.

The office was quiet, as it had been lately. People were out in the field for the most part. There was only one agent in the house; Maggie, who had eyed him from the moment he'd come in.

As soon as Henry sat down, the walls started to close in on him again. His little excursion had done him some good, but it hadn't been enough. The switchboard rang.

"Henry. There's a call for you," Maggie said. He analyzed her voice. She sounded gruff, but that was nothing unusual. It was unlikely to be Gail then, or he would have been able to detect jealousy in her tone.

"Who is it?" Henry asked.

"Your mother." Maggie pressed a few buttons, transferring the call to his desk.

"Hello?" Henry said.

"Son. I need you to come." His mother's voice was low and serious. She didn't sound like her usual, cheerful self. Something was wrong.

"What's happened, ma?" Henry's muscles tensed up again.

"Not over the phone. Just hurry."

The line went dead.

What the hell?

"What was it about?" Maggie asked. There was something in the way she said it that rubbed Henry the wrong way.

He didn't respond, just shook his head. If he engaged her or tried to explain, they'd have another argument. This wasn't the time.

He picked up his coat and rushed out of the building, straight to the Alliance van outside.

He didn't know how fast he drove, or what route he'd taken, but somehow, he reached the farm in record time. His mind had been racing the whole time. What could possibly have happened which she didn't want to tell him during the call? Whatever it was, it had to be bad.

Henry drove up the drive straight towards the front door and slammed his break, causing the van to skid as it came to a halt. Then he ran.

Was she all right? Ever since his dad... His mother was the only family he had left.

He stopped dead in his tracks when his mom opened the front door. She looked just fine. But... she wasn't alone.

Behind her stood two large, shadowy figures. *Shit.* Had Blacke found out what he had been up to and sent in two of his agents to come after his mother?

"What's going on here?" Henry demanded.

"Henry, son. You need to come inside and listen." His mother spoke calmly, which made Henry even more suspicious.

She averted her gaze and stepped aside. Only then did Henry recognize the two men. Matt Argyle and his brother, Jamie, who led the Edinburgh Alliance office.

"What are you two doing here?" Henry asked, uncertain whether they still posed a threat or not.

"I gave them the address," another voice spoke up from further inside the house. Gail.

He'd been had.

"I told you that was it. I can't get involved anymore-" Henry protested. He'd never expected her to fight dirty like this. To involve his own mother in a ruse to meet with him! Although he could now see her more clearly, he refused to look directly at her.

"You're going to want to hear this," his mom interrupted.

Henry shook his head. "No. I promised Maggie. I-"

"Oh, son. I know you're just trying to do right by her. Gail explained what happened already. But what's going on is more important than that."

Henry pressed his lips together and tried to get his anger under control. He did *not* like surprises. And this...

"Jamie, perhaps you'd like to explain."

"My mate, Alison. When I got back from work, she was nowhere to be found."

Henry frowned. *So?* What did that have to do with him?

"She's human," Gail explained. "Blacke had her

brought in."

"Then your office must be involved. Someone must have tipped him off!" Henry speculated.

"No. My people are loyal to a fault."

"Alison is Lee Campbell's daughter," Gail said.

Lee Campbell. Henry knew the name but wasn't sure where from anymore.

"It was Jamie's team that captured Campbell with Alison's help. He's been in the dungeon in Stirling for almost a month now," Gail added.

"Your mate is the daughter of the highest ranking Sons member ever captured?" Henry blurted out. It had all come back to him now. No wonder the name had seemed significant somehow. He shook his head in disbelief. "Okay, well, that's unfortunate, but what did you expect?"

"How dare you," Jamie growled, his right hand going straight for Henry's throat.

"Guys! This isn't helpful," Matt interrupted them, positioning himself in the center of the two angry bears, forcing them apart again.

"The point is, we have the Edinburgh office on our side," Gail said. "The time is right to act. The dungeon is filling up fast, so Blacke's men are transporting Alison to a secondary holding place tonight. With the help of these guys," Gail nodded in Jamie and Matt's direction. "We can take her back without Blacke knowing what - or who - hit him. *If* we make sure we outnumber them."

"Your whole office is ready to oppose Blacke?" Henry asked. With bears being as secretive as they were, how could Jamie be so sure of their loyalties?

"They'll follow me over Blacke, that's for sure," Jamie said.

"So you seem to have everything worked out. What do you need me for?" Henry asked.

"That's very simple. We need you to do nothing," Gail said.

What?!

Scottish Werebear: A Painful Dilemma

If something goes wrong, and Blacke calls for your help to get Alison back, don't come running to his aid. Don't interfere until we have the chance to get away. Gail's voice, no, Gail's entire being had entered his mind.

Henry was stunned into silence by her presence within him. During their short time apart, their connection had become even stronger than on previous occasions. He could even catch glimpses of her memories.

He could see the moment when he'd made that phone call last week. How she'd collapsed onto a cold tile floor and cried.

Henry could feel her heartbreak like it was his own.

Or was it, in fact, his own?

Henry cleared his throat. "I need a moment," he mumbled, and marched down the hall, into the kitchen, leaving the confused brothers and a fragile looking Gail behind.

He'd had this urge before, that deep, all consuming urge to protect Gail, to keep her safe and happy. And of course, he'd done the exact opposite. Henry sat down at the small table where they used to have breakfast when he was a child. This had been his safe place when he was younger.

"Son." His mom shuffled into the kitchen and rested her frail looking hands on the backrest of the chair opposite Henry. "I know you're just trying to do the right thing."

Henry looked up at her. "Whatever I do, I hurt someone."

"Listen to me." She sat down and folded her hands in her lap. "I know you've made a commitment to Maggie. And now you're just trying to stand by that."

Henry nodded. That's exactly what he was trying to do.

His mom got up and retrieved a sheet of paper that had been lying on the kitchen counter. She placed it on the table in front of Henry. "Perhaps it's time to admit you've made a mistake."

Henry's heart sank as he started to read.

Surveillance Recommendation.
Target Name: Helen Weston
Surveillance Mode: Phone Tap.

His signature was there at the bottom, but he sure as hell hadn't sanctioned this!

CHAPTER TWELVE

Gail made sure to keep her distance as she observed the conversation between Henry and his mother. She'd wanted to warn him, but just hadn't had the chance. For that, she was sorry.

She had to feel for Henry, whose mind was racing, running through the various possibilities of how that request had come into being. His thoughts kept circling back to the same conclusion: Maggie. She was the most likely culprit. And then he'd reject his conclusion and rethink.

This went on for a good ten minutes until Gail could no longer stand to watch him struggle within himself.

"It was her, you know," Gail said softly.

"How can you be sure?" Henry turned around, his features tense, determined.

"This is just a print-out, but with the help of one of Jamie's men in the Edinburgh office, we were able to hack into her computer and find the original document. It was right there on her work computer."

"What if someone just used her computer?" Henry slumped back in his chair again with his back towards Gail.

"I know your history makes it harder to accept this, but deep down you already know the truth."

How could she do this? Sanction surveillance against my own mother, her future mother-in-law? Henry's thoughts raged.

Who knows what she was thinking? What's more important is for you to decide how to proceed now, Gail responded.

He sighed and pushed the sheet away from him in disgust. *Was she successful? Did anyone act on this crap?*

We swept the house top to bottom. It's clean. Looks like we intercepted it just in time, Gail replied.

"Very well." Henry pushed his chair back and got up.

His eyes were colder than Gail had ever seen them before. There was nothing more dangerous than a bear who'd been forced into a corner.

He walked right past Gail and marched down the hallway towards where Matt and Jamie were waiting.

"What's the plan?" Henry asked.

Jamie nodded at Matt, then partly turned to include Gail in the conversation.

She'd felt bad about springing this on Henry, but a life was at stake. Alison's life. Blacke had picked her up so he'd have leverage over Campbell during future interrogations. He wouldn't think twice about hurting her - or worse - to get what he wanted.

Now that tempers had calmed, it didn't take long to come up with a plan.

Gail had marked the route on a map, and Henry recognized the road immediately. It ran straight through a dense forest. They didn't want to harm the agents, so they'd lay a trap. If everything went well, they'd get what they wanted without having to resort to too much violence.

———◆———

It was good having Henry back on their side. Gail couldn't help but steal glances at him as he lay beside her in the bushes overlooking the road they'd just blocked off.

Jamie and Matt were hiding just opposite them. And behind the blockade waited two of Jamie's team members; Aidan and Heidi. As he'd said, they didn't think twice about following Jamie into battle against Blacke.

They hadn't been waiting long when a black van approached, its lights bouncing off against the branches of the large tree they'd placed across the road. Breaks squealed as the vehicle came to a stop right in front of the obstacle. There was no way around; they'd made sure of that.

Beside Gail, Henry took a deep breath and put his eye

to the scope of one of the rifles Jamie had provided for the job. It looked like a proper hunting rifle, but took tranquilizer darts instead of live rounds.

Across the road, an owl seemingly called out; the signal.

Henry pulled the trigger, and the agent nearer to him cursed and grabbed for his upper arm. At the same time, another, similar rifle went off, and its dart hit the other agent in the thigh. It took barely a second for the two men to sink to the ground.

They were on.

Gail pulled the balaclava down over her face and jumped across the shrubs they'd been hiding behind. Henry was right behind her.

First, they made sure the agent was knocked out, then they pulled the dart out of his arm and tied his hands with Alliance issue plastic ties they'd retrieved from his own tactical jacket. They would leave as little evidence behind as possible.

Jamie nodded at Gail as he located the keys to the van in the other agent's pocket. He and Matt hurried to the back of the truck and unlocked the door. The two other agents from Jamie's office lifted one of the agents off the street and back into the van.

They were going to hide it in the forest once they were done. It was in everyone's best interest if this ambush remained undiscovered for as long as possible.

Gail watched as everyone did their part. The New Alliance's first act of rebellion.

A sense of pride filled her chest that almost made her forget the ache left behind by Henry's rejection of her. Almost.

She looked at him as he methodically searched the pockets of the agent he'd disabled. They'd confiscate their weapons, communications equipment and anything else that would help the New Alliance.

Their goal was to create a non-violent resistance against Blacke's Alliance, but once he got wind of what they were up to, things could very well escalate. They had to build up a stockpile of weapons. And plus, any gun taken away from these guys meant one gun less for Blacke to aim at their heads if the time came.

Meanwhile, Jamie emerged from the back of the truck, carrying the precious cargo they'd come here for. A red-haired woman, who seemed fast asleep despite all the activity that surrounded her.

"She's been drugged," Jamie whispered.

Gail nodded. "Take her to the farm; she'll be safe there."

The way Jamie looked at the woman in his arms made Gail's knees weak. She'd had her own concerns about Alison's family background, but what she observed now had taken all that away. They were mates. They were meant to be, and at least, Jamie knew it.

As he walked off into the dark forest, the others continued to sanitize the scene. The van was parked off the road and covered in fallen branches. They also dragged the tree back off the road. Then they packed up all their things and headed back to their individual vehicles.

Only Gail and Henry remained.

"Wow, that went well," Gail remarked.

He forced a smile. It was obvious how much he was still struggling with everything.

"What are you going to do now?" Gail asked.

Henry shook his head. "I don't know. I can't tell her that I know about the surveillance request, or she'll turn us in."

Gail wasn't sure how to respond. She wasn't even sure how to act around Henry anymore.

This was too much. His earlier decision to abandon their work together had crushed her. He hadn't done it to hurt her, of course, but that didn't change things. It was difficult, being so close to each other while both their emotions ran so high.

Gail took a moment to breathe in the icy air and

scanned the dark forest that surrounded them. Was that a noise? A rustle? Perhaps an animal out foraging...

No, there was something else out there, something dangerous. Gail could sense it clearly.

"I knew it. I knew he had come out here to see you!" It was Maggie. She was on Gail before the latter had time to react.

Gail's instincts kicked in, and she transformed instantly, but Gail was no match for the much stronger female brown bear.

"Maggie, relax!" Henry called out from the other side of the road. He was with them in less than a seconds.

But Maggie was far from calm. Her paws were on Gail's throat, ready to rip her open if necessary.

Gail tried to struggle free, but it was hopeless. She was stuck. *She's going to kill me.*

No. I won't let her. Henry stared at Gail for a moment, his eyes emitting a reassuring glow. The doubt he'd shown earlier, the conflicted emotions, all of that was gone now.

As desperate as her situation was, Gail trusted him. He'd intervene.

"You promised you'd stop this. Liar!" Maggie hissed at Henry.

"I had. I had given up everything I believed in for you. For us," Henry said.

Maggie snarled. "Bullshit! You couldn't wait to run off again. With *her.*"

Gail closed her eyes and focused on calm, deep breaths. Maggie's claw dug dangerously into her throat, near the jugular. One wrong move and she'd be done for.

"It wasn't like that."

"Good thing I had the sense to put a tracker on your phone, or I would have never known for sure!"

"This is between you and me, she has nothing to do with this," Henry growled.

Maggie didn't respond.

"All I've ever wanted was to make a difference. Why

can't you see that? Why does everything have to turn into a fight with you?" Henry paced around the car as he spoke.

Gail felt Maggie's grip on her tighten.

"I won't accept that. I can't."

"Then deal with me. Leave her alone," Henry straightened himself and started to transform. Fur, claws, teeth all seemed to erupt at once. And his muscles... He stood at least eight feet tall, towering over Maggie and Gail.

Gail had seen plenty of metamorphoses before, including brown bears. But Henry... He was something else.

Maggie flinched at the sight of him, giving Gail the chance to slip out from underneath her grasp. She was free, but her heart was out for blood.

This was the woman who had stood between her and Henry. If she killed her now, she'd just be defending herself. And that problem would be solved forever.

Gail let out a vicious roar and pounced, this time, it was her having Maggie by the throat. She'd rip her to shreds. It would be so easy!

"Stop!" Henry shouted, giving Gail pause. *Don't do it. This is my problem to take care of.*

Gail grudgingly retreated, leaving Maggie lying on her back in the dirt.

Now, it was Henry's turn to attack. He restrained her but took care not to do much damage.

Get the gun. Henry stared at Gail.

He *had* changed. His eyes were no longer cold and impersonal but full of fire. His bear had recognized her at last. Now that this charade with Maggie was well and truly over, he could see the truth she had known from the first time they'd met.

Gail shifted back into her human self and reached for the rifle that had ended up on the ground between them in all the confusion.

Do it.

Gail didn't need to be told twice and shot a tranquilizer dart right into Maggie's shoulder.

Henry turned away from his former mate as her body went limp, and slowly her limbs and body became smooth and hairless again, and what had once been a fierce brown bear had turned into a woman again.

"What do we do with her?" Gail asked.

Henry stared down at Maggie's limp body with disdain. If he'd loved her at some point, Gail could no longer see any evidence of it. Ever the gentleman, he draped some of his torn clothes over her and picked her up.

"We'll work it out later. For now, she goes into the van."

Together, they returned to Henry's van which was parked on an overgrown track just off the road. He got a blanket out of the back and used it to wrap Maggie in, before placing her on top of one of the benches inside. Then he slammed the door shut and got into the front. Gail followed.

They both sat back and gazed out the window at the forest stretching out of them. All seemed peaceful again outside, as though nothing had happened.

"How ironic, that while I was hiding my work here from her, she had her own secrets."

Gail had nothing much to offer in way of support. She smiled bleakly and lifted her hand to squeeze his arm, then changed her mind. This wasn't the time for uninvited physical contact.

No. It's okay, Henry thought.

Gail looked up and found him already staring at her.

This was that look. The one that she'd only seen before in those illicit dreams she used to have of him. *You were right. I was wrong.*

Gail held her breath and did finally place her hand on Henry's arm, actually touching him for the first time. *You're mine. I am yours.*

That's right.

CHAPTER THIRTEEN

Henry couldn't explain how it had happened, but when Maggie had threatened to kill Gail, everything had fallen into place. The dilemma he'd struggled with ever since meeting Gail for the first time had cleared itself up. His feelings of guilt and misplaced loyalty towards Maggie had vanished.

He'd finally achieved complete clarity.

He and Maggie had lived together for two years, sure. But she was not his mate.

Gail was.

And while he'd been in denial, Gail had known it all along.

In trying to do the right thing and act honorably, he'd almost thrown away the best thing that had ever happened to him. He'd hurt her deeply, which he'd regret forever. In trying to not betray Maggie, he'd betrayed himself and everything he stood for as well. He was grateful to get a chance to make up for it.

Henry glanced at her from the corner of his eye as he started the van.

She had an exotic beauty about her. Her skin tone richer than most native shifters. And those eyes, nearly black, that's how dark they were.

Gail met his gaze. Fiery black, did that even make sense? Either way, the intensity with which she looked at him was enough to light a fire under his imagination. The things he could do to her. The possibilities were endless now.

He couldn't take her home. It didn't feel right, with all

of Maggie's things littering the place.

The farm? That would be awkward, with his mom right there.

My place isn't far from here. Gail winked at him and looked straight ahead out the window again.

Henry put the van into gear and drove off, following Gail's directions.

"I'm sorry, you know. For everything," Henry said.

"It's okay. I know you'll make it up to me." Gail rested her hand on top of his.

Henry's chest tightened, his breaths grew shallower. If they didn't reach it soon, he'd have to pull over and act on his impulses right here in the van.

Take the next left, Gail directed him. *It's the house at the end of the road.*

Henry focused once more on the road. Just a little while longer.

Once he'd taken the turn, he could see the house from afar. It was quaint, simple. A brick built cottage, much smaller than most houses they'd passed by on the way.

He parked at the side of the road and got out as fast as he could. Gail was already two steps ahead. They raced each other to the front door. Henry caught her on the last step.

Gail giggled. "Keen, are we?"

"Tell you'd rather have it another way, and I'll tone it down," Henry whispered in her ear.

"No way."

Gail unlocked the door, and they stumbled inside. Henry wrapped his arm around Gail's waist, twirling her around to face him.

The door clicked shut behind them. They were alone.

This wasn't the first time they had been alone, but in a way it was. They were different now - at least he was. This time, they were both on the same page. Henry's true self was no longer in hiding.

He stared into her eyes. The tension between them was electric. How close he had come to never feel this way? *This was it.*

Gail tiptoed to meet him, and Henry leaned down. Her arms wrapped around his neck, and his hands grabbed hold of her hips. They never looked away as their faces came ever closer.

He'd had no hope in hell to resist this woman if he'd ever given himself permission to really look at her before. Gail melted against him, their lips meeting in a kiss that set both their bodies on fire.

How would she like it? Fast, slow?

As their tongues explored one another for the very first time, their minds raced with thoughts competing with each other in intensity. How he wanted her, in any, or every way.

He couldn't keep his hands off her. Her body felt so unlike his own. Soft, pliable, feminine.

Meanwhile, her hands were on a journey of exploration of their own. Up his back, over his shoulder blades, down his sides.

Gail pulled back, leaving him wanting.

No, don't stop! He needed her lips back. They tasted sweeter than anything he'd ever known. Addictive, intoxicating.

Gail smiled naughtily, averting her gaze downwards. She tugged at his collar. *This coat, it's in the way. I want what's underneath.*

Henry shrugged it off, letting it fall onto the floor. Meanwhile, he tugged at the waistband of her jeans. *So are these.*

Gail bit her bottom lip. *Race?*

He'd never guessed she'd be in this much of a hurry, but he liked it. He rid himself of the remainder of his clothes, only stopping to watch her do the same.

More and more of her smooth, flawless skin came into view. He'd want a taste of all of that, eventually.

The scent of her arousal hit him more strongly now, without any barriers in the way. That's when he lost control. He was no longer the same man who had tried to make a rational choice to resist the temptation she offered. He wasn't capable.

This was where they were meant to be; what they were meant to do.

He grabbed her by the wrists and pressed her body up against the wall. Then he dove in, licking, sucking, and nibbling on the side of her neck, her shoulders. Even her earlobes weren't safe from his affections.

She writhed against him. It was as though her body was begging for more. More touches, more kisses, more admiration.

Henry paused for a moment, finding that she'd shut her eyes. She dealt with the sensory overwhelm differently than he did. She had given herself over to pleasure, to him.

He sank to his knees, kissing his way down her ample chest and stomach as he went. She tasted of sweet vanilla, the expensive kind. Exquisite.

She moaned when he reached his destination. His fingers caressed her folds, before following the same path with his lips and tongue. Delicious.

He spread her as best he could with his hands and lapped at her juices, which had started to flow. Her pleasure heightened to dizzying levels. She was ready. He'd make it happen.

Gail cried out his name as he slipped his finger inside her wet slit.

He felt his entire body fill with a light so bright it overpowered everything. As Gail shivered underneath his continued manipulations, her pleasure peaked, spilling over from her being into his.

Henry closed his eyes and joined her on the wild ride of her orgasm. How keenly he could feel it. He could have never imagined this was possible.

She stirred in front of him. He looked up and found she was gesturing at him to get off the ground.

My turn, lover.

He might as well have been hypnotized. From now on, he'd never be able to refuse her anything.

As soon as he stood on his own two feet again, she took his hand and led him through the interior of the cottage until they reached her bedroom. She led him up to the bed and pushed him down onto his back. He went backward, and she followed, crawling on top of him.

Her hands found his hard cock, causing him to tremble.

I want you.

I need you.

I can't wait.

Henry wasn't sure who had formulated those demands, him or her, but it didn't matter.

She mounted him, and he found himself burrowed deep inside her. He knew this feeling. It was like a dream he'd had, which he'd forced himself to forget.

Gail's voice filled the room. Moans, cries. Like music to his ears.

She rode him hard. That first orgasm had done nothing to slow her down.

Amazing, how the reserved Gail he had first come to know had vanished, and been replaced by this free spirit that sought to free him as well now. He wasn't complaining, of course. He reveled in it.

After everything he'd done to her, he hardly deserved this. He didn't deserve her, but here she was.

His body became hot, from the inside out. It was no longer blood that flowed through his veins, but liquid fire. From the farthest points in his body, it all traveled in the same direction, towards his core. And there it pooled until he was so filled with heat, he thought he was going to explode.

Gail showed no exhaustion; instead, she sped up.

He couldn't take it anymore, bucking his hips upwards, into her. They were no longer two people, with differing opinions, opposing dreams.

Henry groaned as his body turned rigid.

They were one.

We are one.

Gail collapsed on top of him, shuddering, as tears streamed down her face.

We are one at last.

As soon as he caught his breath, he embraced her. Gail slipped off him, just far enough to straighten her body. After today, he'd never let her go.

"I love you," Henry said. Strange, saying that out loud. He'd never said those words before, not even to Maggie. And yet, after such a short time as mates, they felt appropriate now.

Gail sighed and rested her head on his shoulder. "I love you too."

They stayed like this for the rest of the night, dreaming, thinking, talking in silence.

For now, they were safe. But their peace wouldn't last long.

Soon, Maggie would wake up. They both agreed that harming a fellow shifter, no matter what she'd done, would be unacceptable.

They'd have to let her go.

She would set Blacke and his men after them.

We've got more people now. The New Alliance has grown significantly these past days.

Exponentially? Like a virus. Henry smiled.

Gail ran her fingers over his lips. *Something like that.*

Perhaps it wouldn't be long then. They'd go into hiding until it was time to come out to the world.

But we won't have anyone inside Blacke's office, Henry suddenly realized.

Oh, but I think we do. Gail lifted herself and gave him a peck on the cheek.

That was that then. Their new plan. They'd be okay, as long as they stuck together.

***

ABOUT THE AUTHOR

---◦◦---

Dear Reader,

Thanks for reading Scottish Werebear: A Painful Dilemma, Book 5 in the Scottish Werebears Series. Although this is my first published paranormal romance series, I'm not new to writing in general. In fact, my mom still tells me to this day about how I would make up stories, and attempt to record them in my clumsy, shaky handwriting from the moment I learned to read and write. From there I went on to write fan fiction and other stuff meant for my own eyes only.

I've always enjoyed stories of the paranormal. Vampires, shape shifters, witches and magic, all featured in the books I loved the most, even when I was still growing up. But it wasn't until much later that I got into romance. One of the first writers (a self-published author just like me!) I came across was Tina Folsom, via her Scanguards Vampire series. I was hooked. From there I went on to read more paranormal romance until I found a new favorite kind of hero: bear shifters, like the kind written by Milly Taiden, Zoe Chant, and T.S. Joyce. What I love about bears is how they can be all strong and independent, a bit reclusive, and almost grumpy, but they always end up having a heart of gold (plus they tend to know their food, and we all know that a man who can cook is doubly sexy). All that (except for the shifting into a powerful bear) almost exactly describes the sort of man I ended up falling for and marrying in real life, so it's no surprise that this is what I started my publishing career with.

To find out more, check:
LoreleiMoone.com (And why not sign up for the newsletter to be the first to find out about new releases.)

You can also get in touch with me via Facebook (search for Lorelei Moone), or email at info@loreleimoone.com

I also write contemporary romance as L. Moone. If that's something you're interested in, you can take a look at LMoone.com.

x Lorelei